RUINED BY THE ROOK

MURDOCH MAFIA SERIES
BOOK 6

SAMANTHA BARRETT

For Clare,
Thank you for loving each of these guys, pushing me to write
more daily, and blowing smoke up my ass daily. You are the
best boost to my ego, I am so glad we met and bonded over
our love of Twilight.
This book is for you, you believed in Rook making a
comeback even when I didn't, so here he is.

AUTHORS NOTE

This book may make some uncomfortable with the content.
I have always sworn if I ever wrote a mafia book, I would go
dark,
in order to stay true to my character's that is what I have
done.
Some scenes and descriptions may make you uneasy,
make you feel squeamish but rest assured there is an HEA.
For those who have read my PNR and thought they were
dark, well this is worse, so much worse but in the best way
possible.

Welcome to the Murdoch Mafia and all their fucked up
shit.

Prologue

Rook

This should have been a story about the youngest sibling being rescued and returned to his family, grateful, happy, and overcome with gratitude to be safe and home again.

What a crock of shit that is.

That isn't how my story goes, I'm not grateful and I sure as fuck am not thankful. I lived in fucking fear for eight months!

Eight fucking months, while my family lived happily, fucked, pro created and carried on like I didn't exist. They expect me to bow to them because they found me, they can all fuck off.

Nah, this isn't some story with a happy fucking ending.

This is the story of how they all came to be *Ruined By The Rook*, especially *her*.

Chapter One

Months have passed and still I sit here silently in my room like every other day. Bishop and the others have forced me to meet with the therapist that Ally and Knight meet with weekly, even Anya speaks with Opal. But not me. I sit there for an hour twice a week and say nothing. Opal never comments, just says, *'I'll listen whenever you are ready.'*. It pisses me off that she never looks bored, never fidgets or looks around the room aimlessly, she just sits there with a smile and fucking waits!

Like right now, she just sits with her pad and pen and smiles encouragingly at me. I don't want to fucking talk. I relive everything that happened each night. I don't sleep. If I do, it's power naps and reading. I never thought I would *ever* willingly pick up a book and want to read but now, it's all I do. Fiction, non-fiction, it doesn't matter to me as long as I get lost in the story and stay out of my own head.

"I want to try something different today." I dart my gaze over her head to peek at the clock and fight the urge to roll my eyes. It's only been ten minutes since I came in here. "I know that Bishop and Kiara got married, so did your sister and Vincent. Carlina and Kiara are both pregnant. Allison and King are being wed this weekend. Your twin has had children of his own, and is engaged. Gage is also engaged. How do you feel about all these big changes in your life?"

I try to sift through my thoughts and actually think about her question. Truth is, I don't know how I feel about any of that. All I feel is anger and bitterness. I know Koby can't stomach the sight of me because she feels guilty. Knight blames himself for me being taken. The thing is, everyone feels some type of way about what happened to me and I hate it! None of them were there, they think saying sorry and telling me they are there for me is going to erase what happened, it won't! Yes, I was spoiled by Bishop growing up and am the baby of the family but now, I don't even recognize the person I used to be.

"That's because you are different now." I cut my gaze to Opal and frown, she smiles encouragingly as she continues. "You spoke aloud just then." I grit my teeth in frustration. "Look, Bishop came to me and asked if I had any suggestions that would help you with your healing journey. I suggested you having your own place might be a good start." Now she has my full attention, if she manages to convince my big bro to let me move out, she is fucking better at her job than I thought. "He agreed."

"What?" The word spews from my mouth before I can stop it. Opal startles but regains her composure quickly.

"Bishop has made the preparations needed but I will

leave that for him to discuss with you. I need you to know, there are conditions for you moving out." My nostrils flare in annoyance, I try to keep my breathing neutral as I grit out.

"What are they?" She smiles like she has won some fucking award.

"You must meet with me three times a week and converse in each session." I shake my head. Her and Bishop think they can threaten me into doing as they like, well newsflash fuckers, I'm not a kid and can do whatever the fuck I like. To prove my point, I flip Opal off and storm out of the room making sure to slam the door behind me hard enough to rattle the pictures on the wall.

"SUCK IT!" I fight the gag that wants to break free and obey, I hate myself for being so weak but what choice do I have? I thought Bishop would have come for me by now, if not him then definitely King. I don't know if Knight would come, I got his girl killed and I can't blame him for hating me for that. "Just like that, dvornyaga (mutt)." If I could kill myself I would. I fucking hate Ivan Volkov and everything he stands for. If he isn't forcing me to blow him, he's fucking me. If it isn't me getting fucked, then he is raping some poor helpless girl in the cell next to me. He forces me to watch, not the act itself but him. He likes it when I make eye contact with him, especially when he comes.

I bolt upright in bed, breathing so fast my head begins to spin. My body is covered in a sheen of sweat. My bedroom door flies open, and I act on instinct. I leap from the bed and huddle in the corner of the room, slamming my eyes closed when the light flicks on. I wrap my arms around my knees and bury my face in the top of them. My body begins to tremble with fear. I fucking hate this part! I know what's coming and I am too fucking weak and powerless to stop the bastard from using me or hurting me. I want it all to fucking stop! Hands grip me, I keep my eyes closed not wanting to see his face as I thrash in his hold.

"Rook!" I know that voice. "It's me, open your eyes." I freeze when the hold on me turns from frantic to gentle. I slowly peel my eyes open and slam them closed as the bright light assaults me. "Open your eyes, brother. You're safe." I follow Bishop's order and slowly blink my eyes open. It takes me a moment to adjust to the light, but when I do I see a panicked look on his face as he kneels in front of me. I look over his shoulder to see King standing in the doorway tugging at the strands of his hair, looking like he wants to break shit. "Shit." I focus back on Bishop who looks stricken. "Let's... get you cleaned up." I'm confused as fuck for a minute. I follow his line of sight and that's when embarrassment and shame courses through me, I fucking pissed myself in fear.

"Get the fuck away from me!" I snarl as I shove Bishop back and push to my feet. I ignore King as I storm past him and head for my bathroom, slamming the door closed and lock it. I grind my teeth in anger and start to punch the door. After the second hit, my knuckles split but the pain is a welcome distraction. When I hear my brother's shouting for me to open up, I step back and shake my head but say nothing. I avoid looking at myself in mirror as I peel off my soiled boxers and chuck them in the hamper before stepping into the shower. I turn the temperature to scalding hot and stand under the spray, loving the feeling of it burning my skin. I grab my loofah and scrub my skin raw trying to cleanse myself of the filth that clings to me. It doesn't matter how long or how hard I scrub, the feeling of being tainted and dirty is still there.

———

BY THE TIME I step out of the shower my fingers are prunes and my eyes are heavy with exhaustion and unshed tears. I'm a fucking man. I shouldn't be sitting in my room crying every fucking day! I see Anya living her best life even after she was raped by her own uncle. Ally smiles nonstop even after what she went through. Koby and Knight are so happy being parents and loving their twins. Bishop and Kiara are happily married and expecting their first kid soon. Even my sister is married and about to have a kid. Then there is me. The family fuck up. The disgrace. The burden.

I need to get the hell out of this house before I lose my mind. Huh, I probably already fucking have. I see things that aren't even there—like I could be reading a book and then all of a sudden I'm back in Russia, chained to a wall and being whipped like a dog. I push away those dark thoughts and step out of the bathroom only to be greeted by the sight of Bishop sitting on the edge of my bed with his face buried in his hands. I throw my head back and fight the groan from breaking free, this is the last thing I want to deal with right now.

"I'm sorry." I lull my head forward and give him a bored look. "I don't know what I'm supposed to do here, Rook. It's been nearly five months since we have been back from Russia and you still won't speak to any of us. I don't know how to fix this if you don't—"

"You can't fix this!" I roar. Bishop doesn't flinch or even shift an inch just stares at me with nothing but guilt in his eyes. Don't they get it, nothing they do will fix what happened. They can't change it! "Get the fuck out ,Bishop. I don't need your bullshit apologies or pity." I watch as he stands silently and walks toward the door. Before he can leave, I say more. "Opal told me about the deal. Let me leave and I'll stick to the arrangement. Use it against me and I'll disappear, except this time, you will never see me again." I watch as his whole body stiffens, his grip on the door handle is so tight he may actually break it.

"I'll always be here, Rook," he whispers.

"Just get me what I want."

"Fine." Now it's my turn to stiffen as he turns around, this time there is no guilt in his gaze only determination. "I'll get you the keys and a house within a couple months." I grit my teeth and nod; I can persevere for another two months. "Before I hand the keys over, you have to meet your nephews. Don't bother arguing with me, Rook. I have this whole fucking place locked down tighter than Carlina's grip on Vincent's balls, you won't get out. Meet them and you'll have your freedom." He doesn't wait for a reply as he slams the door closed behind himself.

Chapter Two

Clare

One month later....

I roll up my sleeping mat and stuff it inside my pack. I stretch and cringe when my back cracks loudly. Sleeping on the ground in the woods of Central Park isn't the best but it will have to do until I can reach Luka. He doesn't owe me a freaking thing but he is all I have left. I grab my belongings and shove them inside my bag before shoving my arms through the straps. It's heavy and weighs me down but everything I own is in this bag. I crouch down and carefully grab the urn, then wrap my arms around it and hold it close to my chest. Nearly six months ago I came out here to get Luka's help. He didn't even give me a chance to explain why I was here before he had one of his guys driving me back to the airport and dumping me on the next flight back home.

I'm mad as hell at him but I don't have anywhere else to go, he's all I have left. Today is the day I go back and make him listen because this time, he can't send me back to Oklahoma.

I don't have a home anymore.

I make my way through Central Park and keep my head down. People in New York don't take kindly to homeless people. The guys think because I'm homeless I'll allow them to make themselves at home inside me for a quick buck! They can fuck right off with that mentality.

I don't have enough money for a cab and my stomach is protesting by growling about not having any food inside it for a couple days. I keep my head down and try not to groan or drool as I walk past a hot dog cart. My stomach begins to cramp, so I hold the urn tighter and push on. I won't reach Luka until nightfall at this rate. It's cold, you can smell snow in the air, so I really don't want to be sleeping in the park when the first snowflakes begin to fall.

BY THE TIME I make it onto the street where the Murdoch's residence is, it was like it got colder, almost like the universe is telling me this isn't a good place. I know it isn't, I've been here before. Not inside the house but outside it, where I met Rook. He wasn't jaded or hateful back then. I was just a kid, fifteen years old and nothing but stars in my eyes thinking the world is a good place. How wrong I was. Halfway down the street I pause, there never used to be a gate here. With my hands free and the urn safely in my pack, I grip the bars and try to squint my eyes to get a better view of the houses. This place has changed so much over the past four years.

Now there are more houses either side of the street with the main one still the furthest back. It looks daunting from way back here. Rook told me that house wasn't a home, it was a prison. I didn't understand what that meant. I came from a loving home. My step mom was amazing. My mom died during childbirth so I never got a chance to get to know her. I never felt like I was missing out though, Lillie never made me feel like I wasn't her own. My dad, he was my best friend, I could tell him anything and he would never get mad. He never raised his voice or spanked me, even when I told him I was pregnant at fifteen.

"Step away from the gate!" I yelp and jump back scared shitless at the sudden appearance of a man dressed like a security guard. He narrows his eyes. "Go beg for scraps somewhere else, kid." I scowl at the beefed-up juice head, whose shirt looks two sizes too small for him.

"I'm not a beggar, you nitwit!" Beefy grits his teeth, clearly pissed now.

"Get the hell out of here now!" he roars. I clench my hands into fists so he doesn't see them shaking. I know Luka works for the mafia and I should have thicker skin, but I was never exposed to this type of stuff. I lived a really sheltered life.

"No. I need to speak to Luka." His brow furrows, clearly taken back by my request.

"Why would he want to see poor pussy like you?" I cringe and fight the retort that wants to break free as he rudely spoke to me.

"One, eww. Two, because I'm his little sister." Beefy's eyes widen a fraction before he schools his features.

"Where's your proof?" My jaw unhinges, he cannot be serious.

"How the hell am I going to prove that?"

"Call him." I cringe, it's a simple request but one I can't do.

"I don't have a phone," I mutter under my breath embarrassed, he scoffs.

"Nice try, kid. Get the hell out of here." Desperation crawls through me. I lurch forward and grip the bars looking at him hoping he can see the truth in my eyes.

"I swear, Luka Salinski is my brother."

"And I'm the fucking Pope. Fuck off now before I make you." He turns to leave and all hope flees me until I hear his voice.

"You gonna lay hands on a little girl, Chris?" I stand up straighter and search for him in the darkness but I can't see him.

"Whose there?" Beefy calls out, his hand goes to his hip to grip his... gun. Oh my God. He has a freaking gun!

"You pull that gun and I will be the least of your worries." He steps out from the shadows of the trees that line either side of this fence line, my breath hitches. He looks like a dark angel standing there in dark jeans and a black sweater with the hood pulled over his head. I can't see his face and it bugs me.

"Shit, sorry, Rook. I had no idea you were out here. Did you need something?" Rook turns his head toward me. I may not be able to see his eyes but I can feel them when my body begins to burn with awareness. I can feel him looking me over and it sends a shiver down my spine.

"Let her in," he says while keeping his dark gaze on me. The guy pushes some buttons on a hidden keypad, then the gates begin to open. I try to move but a feeling of uncertainty thrums through me. I don't know how I know this, but if I step through those gates I feel like my life will change forever.

What other option do you have? the little voice in my head says. I take a deep breath, square my shoulders and take the first steps into what I am sure is going to be my new life. Rook doesn't wait for me, just turns and heads toward Murdoch Manor as I call it. Neither of us say a word on the walk, with him staying at least five steps in front of me. I try to get a look at each of the houses but it's pretty hard when it's dark out and there are no street lamps. There are three large houses either side of the street with the seventh being the Manor. Who the hell lives this close to them? I'm too lost in my own thoughts to notice Rook has stopped moving and crash into his back with a grunt escaping me. I stumble backward as he turns to face me. A gentleman would reach out and help steady me on my feet but not Rook. He stares at me like I'm the bane of his existence.

"Thanks for the assist," I grumble. He doesn't comment for a long while, just stares at me in the most unnerving way which causes me to fidget. The intensity of his stare has my body heating with awareness. I hate that even when he looks at me like I am nothing he can draw this type of reaction from me. "Where's Luka?" I finally ask, breaking the tension-filled silence.

"Why'd you do it?" His voice is quiet but I can hear the undertones of his rage simmering just beneath the surface. I don't pretend to act like I don't know what he's talking about. I don't want to have this conversation right now but it doesn't look like I have a choice. I grip the straps of my bag for something to hang onto as I relive the darkest moment of my life. Rook thinks I ran from him because of the baby, but he is so wrong.

"I didn't have a choice," I whisper, tears build and I slam my eyes closed to keep them at bay. Only my dad and Rook knew about the baby. We moved to Oklahoma before Luka knew a thing about me and Rook.

"Don't you stand there and fucking cry like a pussy. This is all your fault!" I snap my eyes open and peer up at him, taken back by his remark. He is vibrating with anger. Now that we stand at the base of the steps of the Manor, the outside lights illuminate his features. His eyes are so dark and filled with so much pain. "I fucking hate you!" I recoil not from his words but from how loud he is shouting. "You fucking ruined everything. If you'd never left, none of this would have happened." Utterly confused and dumbfounded at what he is saying, I just shake my head denying his claims. "You fucking ruin everything, everything you touch gets ruined." Tears fall from my eyes, I'm powerless to stop them. He has no idea that his words hit so close to everything I have tried to hide from.

"That's enough, Rook!" I jump in fright. I look to the side to see Rook's twin, Knight standing there with his older brother, King and another guy who looks like them. Do they have another brother? Knight looks between Rook and me. I can see from the way he is studying me he has no idea of mine and Rook's history.

"Stay the fuck out of this," Rook growls. I gasp and stumble back a step shocked that he moved so close and I didn't even hear him.

Chapter Three

Before she can take another step, I snap my arm out and grip the back of her neck, pulling her in close to me but still keeping an inch of space between us. Her eyes are wide and full of fear. Good, she should be fucking scared. She could have stayed and rewrote the outcome of my life. She could have changed the path I was on if she had just stayed, maybe then I wouldn't have ended up in Russia. I hear King, Knight and Gage rush toward us. If they are smart they won't fucking lay a single hand on me or *her*. For the first time in fucking months since I came back, I finally feel something other than despair and self-loathing. I feel fucking rage and an insane urge to ruin Clare Santiago in every way possible.

"Let her go, brother." King and Knight stand on either

side of me but keep a foot of space between us. They have learned to give me space or risk me flipping out and landing a solid punch to their faces. Gage stands behind Clare, lifting his hand, ready to pull her back. I pin him with a look, daring him to lay a single finger on her and risk facing my wrath. "Rook, whatever she did we can sort it out. Just let her go, brother." Since when did Knight become such a fucking pussy. He used to love this shit and now that he's with Koby, he's all noble and shit.

"Clare?" She turns her head toward the house, well as much as my grip will allow. My hold on her tightens when relief shines in her eyes at the sound of Luka's voice. "What the fuck. Let her go!" he shouts. I hear him running toward us. I let up and he pushes in close, knocks my arm away and wraps Clare in his arms. King and Knight form a blockade when I attempt to reach for her again. I shoot each of the fuckers a glare. I used to love each of my siblings with every fiber of my being but now, I feel nothing but rage when I look at them. "Are you okay? What are you doing here?" My nostrils flare in annoyance at the concern in Luka's voice. His sister is a fucking viper, nothing can hurt that snake.

"I'm fine, I needed to talk to you," she says.

"That's what a phone is for, Clare. Dad is going to be worried sick!" She pulls out of his hold and shakes her head, devastation is written across her face. "Just because you're nineteen doesn't mean you—"

"Luka, stop!" she cuts in, slips free of her bag and sets it on the ground. My face contorts in confusion when she pulls out a sleeping mat. The fuck would she need that for? But what stuns me more is when she pulls out a silver urn, wraps her arms around it protectively and stares up at her brother with tears falling freely down her cheeks. "He won't be worried or care because he's here with me." Luka stumbles back a step, shaking his head rapidly.

"No. That can't be, no. I just... I spoke to him like—"

"Nearly five months ago. I came here that first time to tell you he was sick but you wouldn't listen!" Her voice raises on the last part, Luka has turned pale and is clearly in shock. Clare sniffles before carrying on. "You weren't there! He was sick and I needed you."

"You should have called!" he shouts at her. I inch forward ready to... defend her if he lashes out but Knight and King block my path again.

"I tried. You never answered or called me back! What was I supposed to do?" Sobs claw their way out of her and a pang of regret hits me right in the chest. I grit my teeth and push that feeling away. She doesn't deserve my pity, she deserves to wither in pain. Luka curses and stabs a hand through his hair tugging at the ends. His eyes are rimmed with tears but he's too proud to allow us to see him cry. He begins to pace muttering beneath his breath for a second before continuing. Clare hugs her father's ashes tighter, her chin resting against her chest. Her shoulders shake from her silent tears. Gage steps forward and wraps an arm around her shoulder pulling her into his side. It takes everything inside me not to rip his fucking arm off her and beat the shit out of him.

"Take the rest of the night off, you and—" Luka turns to King and shakes his head, then looks to Clare for a second with remorse in his gaze before turning back to him.

"I can't. I have to meet Bishop at the docks for the arrival of the new shipment from Andreas." Clare doesn't look up or make any sudden movements to acknowledge that her brother abandoning her when she needs him most affects her. Luka is a fucking idiot, I know what it's like to be abandoned by your siblings. You live in pain daily while they go about their lives like you never existed!

It fucking stings like a bitch.

I LAY HERE on my bed, one arm resting behind my head and the other draped across my abs as I stare up at the glow in the dark stars on my ceiling. As a kid I hated the dark and was too scared to sleep in my own room, so I would sleep in Knight's. When Tony found out I got a good fucking lashing with his belt. That day, Knight came into my room with a ladder and begin to stick these stars to my ceiling. He told me it would give me enough light not to draw our father's attention—we weren't allowed night lights. He told me to count the stars each night until I fell asleep.

I searched for any sign of light, a single star but I found nothing while I was held in that fucking room for months. I hadn't been scared of the dark for years until being locked in that room. I didn't sleep for days. I was in fucking agony from the bullet wounds, I was so disoriented from the pain and the infection I developed in the first few weeks I had no idea where I was or that I was a prisoner—a sharp knock on my door pulls me from my thoughts. I rest up on my elbows and wait to see if whoever it is will enter or fuck off and leave me alone. A dejected sigh escapes me as the door opens. I expect it to be one of my brothers here to pester me again but I'm floored when Koby steps into my room, flicks the light on and closes the door behind herself.

She rests back against the door, crosses her arms over her chest as she looks around my room, it's spotless. I used to be a slob, I never cared if my room was a mess all I cared about was fucking and playing football every Friday night. I loved being QB, maybe in another life I would have been able to live out my dream of going pro and playing in the Superbowl.

"Why'd you do it?" I almost snort at her question, I asked Clare the same thing mere hours ago. I run my gaze over and take in the changes, Koby is beautiful there is no denying that. Her blonde—almost white—hair is piled on top of her head in a bun, her eyes are bright and filled with love, the haunted look she used to carry around with her is no longer present. Looking at her, you would never know she had given birth to twins five months ago. "Don't ignore me Rook, I need to know why you did it. Why did you take my place." I growl in frustration as I swing my legs over the side of the bed and rest my forearms on my thighs. I can't look at her, I can't picture her going through the fucking hell that I went through.

"Just go—"

Before I can finish kicking her out, she cuts me off, her tone is quieter, softer even as she speaks.

"I know what it's like to be a Volkov pet." I stiffen. "I want to say I'm sorry but no amount of apologizing will change what happened to you and frankly, what the fuck does saying sorry do for anyone?" That gets my attention and even brings a ghost of a smile to my lips. "Just... answer me why you saved my life? Believe it or not, Rook, I wished I could have traded places with you—" Now it's my turn to stop her before she can finish that sentence.

"Don't!" I slowly climb to my feet and face her. Her eyes soften with guilt as her gaze falls to my naked chest. Scars can be seen from the bullet wounds. They mar my front and back from being cut deep with a blade or being chained up like a dog and whipped until I passed out from the pain. It takes more strength than I want to admit to say the next words out loud. "I'd never have traded places with you."

"Why?" she whispers. In all the time I have known Koby, this is the first time I have seen her vulnerable. It's not like her and I were ever close, I mean for fuck's sake the night I got shot I dragged her to the docks pretending to be Knight. I thought she was a mole for the Russian's, turns out I was fucking wrong and the mole was Mav.

"Because I should never have taken you to the docks that night. I thought you were using my... brother." She pushes off the door and on instinct I take a step back. She freezes but doesn't comment on my need to keep distance between us.

"He never gave up on you, he never stopped looking for you. When they found that body, he never believed it was you, Rook. Knight never gave up hope that one day he would find you. He swore he would never rest until you were home." Her words ring true but I'm still too angry to care. "When we found out I was pregnant, I was terrified. Knight was scared but for different reasons. He told me he didn't know how he was going to be able to be a father or even be a good dad because you weren't there to pull his head in. I know you are angry and you have every fucking right to be, but my sons are innocent." Her tone is firm, her eyes are no longer soft but hard in warning. "I love your brother and would cause mass genocide for him, but I do not love him enough for his own twin to project his anger onto my sons because he is pissed at their father. You want to hate Knight and be pissy at him, fine. But what you will not do is take that anger out on Havoc and Chaos. Do I make myself clear?"

I look at her in a whole new light. My respect for her has grown tenfold in the space of minutes. Koby didn't come in here to plead for my brother, well maybe a little, but I respect her for not pushing that issue. So for that reason, I answer her first question.

"I saved you because Knight wouldn't have survived losing you, Koby. I knew he was falling in love with you the second he wouldn't let me join in when I walked in on you. My brother had only slept with one woman before you." She doesn't seem surprised by my declaration which cements what I already know, Knight loves her enough to let her in. "I freaked out. I thought I was going to lose my brother to you. In my head you were the enemy and I wanted to prove my point, so I took you to the docks. I thought for sure you would break and fight so your cover wouldn't be blown but I was wrong and I paid for that mistake." I grit out the end of that sentence, my hands clench at my sides as I take a few deep breaths to try and ease my anger.

"If you expect me to drop to my knees and tell you how amazing you are, you are outta your damn mind. But what I will say is, thank you. If you didn't save me I wouldn't have been able to have my sons and they are everything to me, Rook. They are your brothers world which is why I'm not asking, I'm telling you to come with me and meet your fucking nephews because they are amazing." I shake my head but she pushes on. "Hate their father but not them. They are innocent and need their uncle. Knight and King have left to meet Luka and Bish, he isn't in the nursery, so now is your chance."

When she turns and walks out the door, my legs act on their own and follow after her. Nerves thrum through me as we make our way down the hallway to the door next to Knight's room, that used to be Car's but her and Vin stay in the pool house now. I pause a couple of steps away and watch Koby walk into the room. It's not because of Knight why I've never touched, held, or even looked at the twins—okay maybe that is part of the reason, but it's mostly the fact I'm fucking jealous that his kids got to live and mine didn't. I never had this issue with getting close to Mela, she was older and I guess at that time I wasn't so in my feelings. But now, I can't seem to get out of my head to embrace my own blood.

Chapter Four

Clare

I've tossed and turned for the past hour, sleep is eluding me.

I decide to give up and hop up from the couch I am currently laying on in their games room. Luka was supposed to be back hours ago and promised that we would talk when we got back to his place. I'm angry at my brother. I needed him tonight and as per usual he chose his job over me. I shouldn't be salty, I know that, but for the past five months I have had to deal with dad's passing on my own. Feeling parched, I decide to go and grab a bottle of water. Kiara told me to help myself. My stomach growls begging for food, Kiara offered to make me something when she helped get me settled on the couch but I was too shy to say yes. I have a headache and I know it is from not eating, but it's not like I have the money for food. I spent all the savings I had from working at the diner to cover dad's funeral costs and I'm still paying off his medical bills. When dad got laid off from work, we couldn't afford our insurance so all his hospital trips, well let's just say I'll be paying that off for the rest of my life.

I creep as quietly as I can through the silent house. Kiara told me that all the rooms are upstairs so I shouldn't wake them by helping myself to the kitchen. Kiara did offer me the guest house since it's apparently empty now but I refused. I already feel like a freeloader sleeping on their couch waiting for my brother. I round the corner hoping I'm going the right way, this house is massive and I could easily get lost in here. I tiptoe through the hallway and turn right. Just before I get to the foyer, a sigh of relief escapes me. I make out the counter and sink. Not wanting to turn a light on and alert anyone to my presence or for them to find me helping myself to their food I decide to forgo turning the light on.

I reach out and brush my fingers along the wall using it as a guide to lead me to the fridge and hoping I don't stub my toe on something. A smile breaks free when I feel the handle of the refrigerator, I pull it open and blink my eyes a couple of times to adjust to the dim light of the fridge. My stomach grumbles loudly in the silent room at the sight of all the food. I bite my lip and mentally berate myself.

Don't steal from the mafia, Clare! I keep repeating that in my head as I grab a bottle of water, but then I spot an apple. It's red and looks so crisp, would they really notice one apple missing?

Screw it! I'm so hungry I throw caution to the wind and grab the bloody apple. I close the fridge door, turn to leave then scream when I see a shadow in front of me. A hand clamps over my mouth, I drop the apple and water to the floor as I'm shoved back up against the fridge. I'm frozen with fear, unable to lift my arms and fight back against my assailant. Tears prick the corners of my eyes ready to spill over at a moment's notice.

"If I move my hand you gonna scream again?" I shouldn't sag with relief at the sound of his voice but I do. Rook may have changed *a lot* in the past four years but I know without a doubt he would never hurt me. I nod unable to voice my reply. He drops his hand and moves away. I lose sight of him for a moment but then the light flicks on and blinds me for a second until I adjust to the harsh light. Rook makes his way back to me but this time he leans back against the counter. I'm too frightened to move or even collect the water and apple from the floor. I feel my cheeks heating from the shame of being caught taking food and water from him. I drop my gaze to the floor unable to look at him.

To my utter horror and embarrassment my stomach lets out a roaring grumble and I cringe in pain from the cramps. I haven't eaten in so long that now each time my stomach grumbles, it causes me pain. I chance a look up at Rook through my lashes, only to find him glaring at my stomach. I cross my arms over my stomach and try to flee but he blocks my path.

"Sit, you need to eat." His tone leaves no room for argument. Me being me though, I want to deny him and not give in but when my stomach protests again, I march my ass around the counter and hop up on one of the stools. I watch Rook silently move around the kitchen, grabbing pans and condiments from the fridge. Soon my eyes betray me and stop watching what he is doing and I start watching *him*. He wears a pair of black basketball shorts and a plain white shirt. His hair is a mess of long brown waves and he keeps flicking his head to keep it out of his eyes. When another strand of hair lands on his forehead I want to reach out and brush it away but don't. The only sounds that can be heard are the clanging of pans and sizzling of bacon—the smell alone has me salivating.

I decide to try and distract myself before I shove him out the way and eat whatever he is cooking raw. "Are you still in school?" He freezes up for a second, then slowly peers over his shoulder at me. His eyes are so haunted and filled with deep rooted pain, I want to reach out and ease his pain, make it my own so I can share some of the burden that is troubling him.

"Nah. High school dropout right here, had... other shit come up." He sounds bitter and almost resentful. He turns back to resume cooking. For some reason I feel compelled to keep talking. Once upon a time I thought this man was going to be my future. I may have only been fifteen but I truly thought we had a connection that would last a lifetime.

"Are you planning on going to college?" A snort comes from him as he turns to face me and pins me with a *are you dense* look.

"Look around, Clare. You are sitting in the house of *the* mafia family of New York." I gulp loudly but refuse to allow myself to fidget in fear, his father is no longer here! "Do you really think someone like me could go to college?"

My brows raise in surprise. "Rook, you can do anything you want. Just because your family... has this type of job doesn't mean you have to follow in their footsteps." He shakes his head in disbelief.

"You know, four years ago I would have believed that but now, I can't trust a fucking thing that comes out of your mouth." His harsh words have me recoiling and feeling guilty. I shouldn't feel guilt when what happened was out of my control. He never came after me!

"You can think what you want about me but my statement remains true. You are not bound to walk the same path as your brothers. You were born to be different."

"No, I wasn't born to be anything more than a burden." I snap my gaze to him in shock. "I am the family fuck up. It used to be Knight but I stole the crown from him without even trying." He tries to feign humor but the undercurrent of shame is present in his tone. He turns and piles food onto a plate before sliding it across the counter to me. He opens the drawer and slides a knife and fork to me next. My mouth waters at the sight of bacon, scrambled eggs, grilled tomatoes and mushrooms. I don't bother continuing our conversation, my mind is too sidetracked by the sight of this amazing meal to even form a coherent thought.

I scarf the food down so fast I have to sit up straight and pat my chest to help swallow. I drag in lungfuls of air before I dive in and finish the rest off. It may be a simple meal but right now, I would swear it's something as good as Gordon Ramsey would make. Rook leans against the counter watching me silently. Normally it would bug me that someone is staring at me while I eat but not tonight. Tonight I am going to enjoy this meal and not care what *he* thinks of me. There used to be a time in my life that all I cared about was what Rook Murdoch thought of me. Now, I don't care what anyone thinks. I got my GED online, I didn't have the luxury of going to school while caring for my sick father but I still made it work.

"When was the last time you ate?" I finish my last mouthful before slowly lifting my gaze to his accusing one. I want to lie but something in the way he is looking at me tells it would be a bad idea.

"A few days." His only response is to grunt and glare at my empty plate before turning and storming out of the room. I sit here open-mouthed and shocked as hell at his reaction. I wait a couple minutes thinking he may return but of course, he doesn't. Resigned to my fate I get up, clean up and then head back to my designated bed for the night and wait for my brother. I try to wait for Luka to return but when the sun begins to crest the horizon, I finally lose my battle and fall asleep. Luka never showed.

Chapter Five

Rook

It's around four in the morning when I hear Bishop and Kiara arguing. It's not like their normal fights. Bishop sounds scared and that is the only reason I drag my ass out of bed and peek into the hallway. I look across the hall to see Knight and King doing the same thing as me. The three of us stare at Bishop's closed door at the end of the hall listening to him beg Kiara to tell him what to do. Their bedroom door flies open and an irritated Kiara pins the three of us with a look. We all know that look. Bishop is working her last nerve and she is about to explode. Bishop stands behind her, pale and looking scared. Knight, King and I all exchange worried glances until Kiara speaks.

"Can one of you drive us to the hospital?"

"Why? You gonna kill my brother?" King's jest is met

with a glare from the tiny raven haired beauty. Bishop is still yet to utter a single word.

"No dumbass, but if I don't get there soon he may kill you if I have our baby on the floor." Two point five seconds is all it takes for her words to sink in and the shock to wear off., King and Knight both scramble to change and offer to drive them. Me, I just stand here and watch. I don't offer to help carry bags, offer my brother or Kiara any good lucks or congratulations because, why the fuck would I? I was locked up and treated like a dog and here my brother was fucking his wife and making a baby. So, I do the only thing I can, close my door and get my ass back to bed.

KNOCK, *knock.*

You have got to be shitting me!

It can't be more than twenty minutes since Bishop, King, Knight and Kiara left for the hospital. I heard them call Luka to bring the car around, so I know he would have drove them, which means, the knocking can only be coming from one of the girls. A part of me wants to ignore it but then another part of me, the part that still cares and wants to protect them, wins out. I get my ass out of bed again and yank the door open. I keep the surprise off my face when it isn't one of the girls, it's Vincent looking exactly like Bish did. I sigh and run a hand down my face, he opens his mouth but I beat him to it.

"Let me guess, Car is having the baby and you need a ride because everyone else left with Bishop?" Vincent just nods. I want to slam the door in his face but when I hear a gut wrenching cry come from downstairs and watch Vin's face contort in pain like he is feeling everything my sister is.

"I know you have your own shit, Rook, but I am asking you as her brother to please help me. She is too early and shouldn't be having the baby for another month. Help me, please." His eyes implore me to not shut him out. I may fucking hate this world but Car is the only one who had no idea I was even missing until it was too late.

"Give me two minutes to change and I'll be down there. Get her in my truck." Vin nods his thanks and takes off to do as I asked. I quickly change and swallow some toothpaste before grabbing my wallet and keys, then rushing out the door. I make it to the garage in record time. I jump into the driver's seat and freeze when I see Clare sitting next to me. "The fuck are you doing in here?" I snap.

"Can we go!" I flinch at the sound of Carlina's pain-riddled voice. I open the garage door and start the truck. I'm already flying out of there before the door is fully open. I drive past my soon to be house and grit my teeth. Bishop is fucking around and not giving me any of the keys because he says there are issues with the plumbing. He's full of shit. Opal, the dirty fucking snitch, hit a nerve with me so I stopped talking to her. I know she told Bishop and now he is holding the keys to my freedom in his grasp just to fuck with me. "Babe, I'm scared." I hear Car whisper. I white knuckle the gear shift hating that she is in pain and I can't help her.

"I'm right here, Gucci. I'm not going anywhere, baby." I don't know Vincent but from what I have seen, he seems okay. The way he watches my sister and how he looks at her like she is his reason for breathing is the only *reason* I didn't slit his throat. I know Vincent loves her and Carlina is just as in love with him. I chance a look at them in the rearview mirror, the fear I saw in his eyes earlier is gone. He's hiding his own worries so Car doesn't freak out more.

"What if... what if something is wrong with the baby?"

Car whispers. I see Vin tense in the mirror, he has no idea how to answer that without lying to her.

"Then we are going to the best place." I frown and peer over at Clare. She's leaning around the seat so she can smile at Car. "Your baby is going to be fine. It's safe to deliver a child after thirty-seven weeks. You're just that now, so baby will be fine." I tune out the rest of their conversation and grip the steering wheel in a vice like grip picturing it's Clare's throat.

VIN CALLED AHEAD to the hospital, so when we pull up nurses are already waiting out the front for them with a wheelchair. Once Vin places Car in the wheelchair he pops his head back in my truck.

"Thank you, I owe you one, Rook." He closes the door and takes off after his girl. I don't stick around. I pass King's car on our way out and don't even feel an ounce of guilt for not going to check on Bishop. Fuck them. They carried on without me so I'll do the fucking same. Clare and I don't say a single word to each other the whole way back. I have nothing to say to her. She is the reason I acted out. When she left without so much as a note, I lost it. I stopped caring about everything. I never took anything seriously again. The whole world was a joke to me. Clare Santiago is the only girl I have ever loved and she broke my fucking heart into a million pieces. I wanted to run away with her, start a new life away from this fucked up one where you have to carry a gun.

"I never meant to," she whispers. I look over at her, her head is down and she twiddles with her fingers in her lap.

"What?" I snap. She still won't look up.

"You said what you were thinking out loud." I grind my teeth annoyed at myself for letting that shit slip out.

"Yeah, well, we all make mistakes and you were my biggest one." I make sure my voice doesn't waiver as I say the words. I know it's a lie but when she recoils and sniffs, I know I'm prick for hurting her. The only time I ever feel something other than self-loathing is when I'm around her as I get to unleash all the pent-up rage.

<hr>

"LIFT your fucking guard or next time I'll take the shot and put you on your ass!" Gage doesn't get it, I want him to take the shot. We've been in the ring for hours. He thinks he's training me and helping me focus my anger but truth is, I'm only here because I want to black out. I've figured out that when I get angry enough, I black out and my rage takes control of my body. When I finally come to, my opponent is on the ground and for five blissful minutes I get to feel numb. Gage strikes again and I don't even attempt to dodge. His right hook clips my jaw but not enough to hurt, he pulled his punch.

I scowl at him, the fucker has the cheek to glare back at me. "Fucking pussy, stop pulling your punches!" I sneer. He shakes his head and begins to remove his gloves which sets to piss me off.

"I won't do it," he says but won't meet my gaze.

"Do what?" Once he's removed his gloves he tucks them under his arm and finally looks at me, no sign of pity just... understanding which throws me.

"I won't beat the shit out of you just so you can feel better. You want to fight and go numb then do it in the underground." I scoff.

"Bishop won't allow that." The bitterness that coats my words can be heard.

"Bishop doesn't run the underground, *I do*." That has my attention piqued.

"You'd go against the Don?" I mock. Gage and Bishop haven't fought once since we returned, I'm calling his bluff.

"What can he say when I hand over the gym and the underground to you!" I furrow my brow confused. Gage loves this gym, he would never just give it up. "Anya and I need to travel every couple months and I don't have the time between helping her and the family with everything to run this place." I eye him skeptically.

"You'd hand it over, just like that?" He shakes his head, I knew it was too good to be true.

"Not just like that. I'll teach you how to do the book-keeping and bookings for the underground. This place isn't just about fighting and training, at the end of the day it's a front to launder money, but to me it was my home." I can hear a hint of sadness in his tone at giving this place up. Before Bishop welcomed him into the family, this place was all he had. He was free of the burden that this family lays on you from the moment you take your first breath.

"Why?" I ask.

"Why what, Rook?" I shrug my shoulders and begin to remove my own gloves.

"You had this place and none of the other shit could touch you while you weren't a Murdoch. Why would you give it up?" He smiles proudly and closes the space between us, lays a large on my shoulder as he meets my gaze. I see nothing but love.

"Because all of you were worth the sacrifice." That right that has me fucking floored. "I didn't want the money or the title, I just wanted to be a part of *your* lives, that's it. I would do anything for this family and I mean anything."

"Why?" I whisper.

A sad smile touches his lips. "Believe it or not, little brother, you're worth it." His words may ring true but if I was really worth anything to the others, they would have stopped their lives to try to find me, not move on.

Chapter Six

I am so freaking pissed at my brother!

Luka still hasn't made an appearance. Gage brought a phone to me earlier and told me it was from Luka. I have been pacing the length of the games room I slept in last night, waiting for the damn thing to ring. The house is quiet except for the occasional cry of one of the babies. I saw the little girl I know to be Amelia thanks to Kiara swimming with her mom, but aside from that I haven't seen anyone else. I haven't even seen Rook since he dropped me off and sped away again hours ago. I'm getting more and more annoyed the longer I wait for this freaking phone to ring. I don't know the passcode so I can't unlock it and call Luka. I know I'm the reason he and I don't really talk much anymore, I didn't have a choice. When the *incident* occurred, Dad and I didn't waste time, he and I packed up and moved.

Luke felt betrayed and I still feel guilty about that but the truth is, I couldn't tell him the truth why we left because then his life would have been in danger and that isn't something I could have lived with. The phone rings and startles the hell out of me to the point I nearly drop it. I quickly answer it and hold it to my ear.

"Hello?" I hesitantly answer, I assume it's my brother but I don't want to be presumptuous either.

"Why haven't you called me?" The fact Luka sounds pissed at me just further causes my ire to grow.

"I could ask you the bloody same thing! I'm not the one who left you in some stranger's house alone."

"You didn't give me much of a choice, Clare. I have to work." I can hear the anger that lurks beneath his calmly delivered words.

"I'm so sorry our dad died and it caused your work schedule to fuck up."

"Not *our*, your father died, Clare." I smack my hand over my mouth to stifle my gasp, tears build and I fight to keep them at bay. "Shit! I didn't mean that Clare—"

"Yeah, you did," I whisper through my tears. Luka and I aren't even related by blood. Lillie was his mother and my step mom. My father isn't Luka's biological father, but my dad loved him like he was his own son.

"Look, I'll be back as soon as I can and we can hash this shit out, okay?" Too tired and spent to fight, I agree. I don't want to continue to have this wedge between us anymore. "Clare?"

"Yeah?"

"I want to know the truth about why you and Dad up

and left in the middle of the night." I take a shuddering breath and nod even though he can't see me.

"O-okay," I stutter as fear begins to claw its way up my spine.

"I love you, Clare-bear." Hearing those three words and my childhood nickname come from my brother has me softening and sighing in relief. We're gonna be okay.

"I love you too." Luka ends the call and I flop onto the couch feeling lighter then I have in months. I'm so grateful that even with both our parents gone, Luka didn't cast me aside.

"How cute." I lurch off the couch and spin toward the door. My breaths are coming in rapid pants thanks to Rook scaring the hell out of me.

"You scared me." His eyes crinkle at the corners and a sinister look overshadows his handsome face. He lazily strolls toward me, like a moth to a flame I'm stuck rooted to the spot unable to escape the pull I feel toward him. I want to hate Rook, blame him for my life being ruined but it's hard to hate someone when you're head over heels in love with them. He leaves a sliver of space between us, causing me to crane my head back in order to meet his angry stare. He grips the back of my neck, drawing a sharp breath from me, then bends down until we are eye level. His breath fans across my face causing a shiver to roll through me.

"Why the fuck are you here?" His angry words have me wanting to shut down and hide. He was never this cruel toward me before. He was kind, gentle, loving even, but now, he's cold, ruthless and... mean.

"I had to see my brother." He raises a single brow mockingly.

"See, you never once mentioned Luka was your brother when I was burying my cock inside you every night for months." I flinch at the harsh way he describes our nights together, he's making them out to be dirty and wrong when they weren't. I grit my teeth in frustration to try to tamper the anger that has flared to life inside me.

"You don't get to speak about those times like that, they were sacred and——"

"A fucking mistake." My eyes widen and I gasp. I search his gaze trying to find a flicker of something that shows me he doesn't mean what he said, but I... can't find any. I grip his shirt and don't miss the way he flinches. He can try and hide his reaction but I felt it.

"We may have been a lot of things but a mistake was never one of them." An evil glint enters his gaze, then leans in closer until his lips ghost over mine.

"You are and always will be my biggest regret in life." The fact he can deliver such cruel words without remorse stuns me. He releases me with a slight shove, looks down at me and scoffs in disgust. "How my dick got hard at the sight of you I'll never know. You're fucking filth."

I have two choices, cry or latch onto my anger. I choose the latter.

"And you're a piece of shit that hides instead of dealing with their emotions like you always have!" As soon as the words are out of my mouth, I instantly regret them. I have no idea what he went through. I just assumed it was really bad because of the change in him. Rook is like a viper, he strikes out so fast I don't have time to prepare. His hand wraps around my throat and then we're both falling onto the couch with him on top of me. I freeze beneath him, unable to move. Not just from the weight of his body but from the fact of having him this close to me again is bringing feelings to the surface I thought I had buried and gotten over.

He may be clouded in darkness nowadays, but I can still see a small glimmer of the brown-haired boy with the goofiest smile and brown eyes that shone with nothing but love and wonder. That memory is wiped away when he gets right in my face, our noses touch, not in a soft gentle way. He pushes hard enough against my nose to have tears clouding my vision. I bite down on my lip to keep from crying out in pain.

"You think just because we fucked around for months that you know anything about me?" The malice in his voice can be felt but I refuse to back down. I won't let him treat me like dirt because he is hung up on the idea of punishing me.

"I knew everything there was to know about you, and you knew me better than anyone," I whisper. His eyes spark with the promise of pain, I know whatever he is going to say is going to hurt me worse than anything his father ever did, so I do the only thing I can think of.

I kiss him.

The moment my lips touch his, he turns to stone above me and I know without a doubt I fucked up. My point is proven when his eyes glaze over like he has just retreated so far inside his own mind that he isn't even really here. I pull back in the hopes that putting some space between him and me that he will snap out of it. Nope, he's still not coming back. I attempt to shift out from beneath him but my sudden movement seems to spark life back into him, but not in the way I hoped.

His face contorts in a mix of fear and fury then his hand is around my neck, his grip is so tight my airways are immediately blocked. My eyes are wide with terror, I claw at his arms and face trying to get him to let go but Rook isn't seeing me, it's like my kiss pushed him into a nightmare.

"I'll fucking kill you! You'll never touch me again you fucking Russian cunt," he screams and spittle hits me in the face, my head grows dizzy from lack of oxygen, my vision begins to grow unfocused and I know I have mere seconds before I pass out.

"Rook, no!" Is all I hear before everything goes black.

Chapter Seven

He'll never fucking touch me again.

I'll kill him, that will solve it all. I just need to hold on for a few more seconds and then my nightmare will be over, Ivan will be gone for good!

"Rook, no!" I hear a voice shout but whoever it is sounds so far away. I know that voice though. Why is my brother here? No, no, no! He can't be here, I can't let that fucker get my brother, not Knight! Arms wrap around me but I fight them off, Ivan has to die. "You're killing her!" Is the last thing I hear before I'm sent careening through the air and land on my ass with a resounding oomph. The foggy haze I was under starts to clear and my vision begins to sharpen once again, horror fills me at the sight I see.

"What the fuck have I done?" I rasp out to no one.

Knight kneels beside the couch checking Clare's pulse as I look down at my hands with absolute disgust. I fucking hurt her! I'm angry as hell at Clare but I would never want to cause her harm, not like this.

"She's alive," Knight says as he peers over his shoulder at me. I see the look of alarm in his eyes and it grates on my nerves. I don't know what the fuck just came over me! Knight scoops Clare into his arms and stands. I jump to my feet ready to stop him from fleeing with her but clamp my mouth closed when Luka walks in. His eyes widen when they land on his sister. He rushes forward and checks her over for any sign of obvious injury. He won't find any, when she wakes every ounce of pain she feels will be in her throat. If he looks hard enough he'll see the bruising starting to take shape on her neck. Self-loathing fills me and I drop my gaze to the floor unable to look at her any longer knowing I'm the reason she lays in my brother's arms unconscious.

"What the fuck happened to her?" Luka shouts. I fight the flinch that wants to break free.

"It was an accident, he didn't—" Luka doesn't give Knight a chance to finish. I don't blame him when he comes for me, grips the front of my shirt and shoves me back until I smack against the wall.

"The fuck did you do to my sister, Rook?" he shouts in my face. I've seen Luka pissed off and angry before but never like this. Do I blame him though? Not one fucking bit. I would be doing exactly what he is if that was Car. What I don't expect though is to hear guns cocking. I dart my gaze toward the entryway and I'm immediately taken back by the sight.

"Step away from him now!" Anya and Koby both stand there with guns drawn and pointed at Luka. I'm shocked that both of these two would be here ready to defend me. I wasn't exactly *friendly* with Koby and did accuse her of playing us. Anya, I have no idea why she is here when I don't even know her. She should hate me, I saw everything that was done to her and did nothing to stop it. I couldn't. I was too fucking weak and petrified of my own shadow.

"Babe, where are the boys?" Knight doesn't reprimand his girl or tell her to drop the gun, he's more worried that she left their sons unattended. Koby grabs a monitor looking thing from her back pocket without taking her eyes off Luka and waves it in Knight's general direction.

"Nap time, playboy." Knight nods. "She better have been in danger for her to be in your arms." I don't miss the underlying threat in Koby's voice. She may be engaged to my twin and the mother to his kids but she is still clearly possessive as fuck over my brother. Knight gently lays Clare on the couch before making his way over to his girl, I hate the look in his eyes. He stares at her like she makes all his demons disappear.

"She, uh, passed out and I was just helping, I swear." Koby darts her gaze to Knight, gives him a once over before reluctantly accepting his answer.

"Step away from him now, Luka," Anya growls. He doesn't listen. He keeps his gaze laser focused on me. I don't miss the warning I see in his eyes.

"You will stay the hell away from my sister." Now that has all my emotions taking a back seat and allowing my anger to seize control of the situation. His grip on my shirt tightens as I push my forehead against his and maintain eye contact. I allow him to see the rage that simmers just beneath the surface.

"She's the one who keeps coming back for more, Luka." He presses his head against mine harder drawing a gleeful smirk from me at the possibility of finally being able to go a round with the Don's pet. Bishop has never allowed Luka to fight in the underground, only that pussy-ass bitch Mav.

"Touch her against her will again and not even your brother will be able to save you from me," he snarls. The prospect of fighting him fuels a beast inside me that thrives off the misery of others. If he thinks the thought of pissing Bishop off will stop me, he's wrong. I want to fuck with everything those bastards have built, I want to watch my fucking family burn and wallow in the misery that I do every fucking day!

"L-Luka?" At the sound of his sister's raspy voice, he releases me with a hard shove. I watch him scoop her off the couch and march out of the room. Clare meets my gaze over her brother's shoulder, I expect to see hatred in her green eyes but instead all I see is understanding and that has my mind reeling.

***

LAYING out here next to the pool on one of the loungers staring up at the night sky is the only source of peace I seem to find these days. It's not often my mind is quiet, some nights I come out here just to remind myself I'm not stuck in that dark fucking room anymore. I'm free to come and go as I please. I used to hate being alone, never liked silence, and yet I now crave it. I crave the peace being alone affords me, well, I did until that dirty little life drainer came back. Clare Santiago was my first love, my first everything. The night she ran from me, she tore my heart out and stomped all over it. At the sound of the back door opening I lull my head to the side to see Knight. I blow out a frustrated breath at the sight of him

"I know you hate me," I snort in answer to his stupid as

fuck observation. Out of all my siblings, he's the one who I blame the most. I hear his footsteps grow nearer and I prepare myself for the confrontation that has been months in the making now that Bishop, Gage and King aren't here to stop it. They're still at the hospital with Kiara and Car—from what I heard they both had their babies earlier today. "What is it going to take, Rook?" I turn and peer over at him. He sits there facing me with his arms dangling between his legs, dark circles under his eyes from lack of sleep. I should feel sorry for him but I don't. I love knowing he doesn't sleep either. I hope his guilt plagues him nightly like my nightmares destroy everything good I try to find in my life.

"For what?" I snap in a flat tone. He sighs and runs a hand down his face. It's then I notice just how much he has changed. He isn't tense anymore, his eyes don't hold that haunted look they used to. He even smiles now and it's weird for me to see him interact with Koby. Fuck, just knowing he is a dad weirds me the fuck out. Knight never wanted a girlfriend or kids, he always said that he would just father the tribe of kids I had.

"For you to forgive me and let me the fuck in? I'm trying here, brother, but you keep shutting me the fuck out—"

"Because I don't fucking need you!" I snarl as I drag myself up into a sitting position to face him, my fists clenched at my sides. I attempt to take some calming breaths. The anger inside me wants me to lash out and give a dose of some of the pain I felt, just a smidge—but another part of me knows it wrong. The anger wins. "You think you can come out here and act like you care—"

"I do fucking care!"

"Bullshit!" I seethe. We both jump to our feet, leaving only an inch of space between us. I stare at him and fight the flinch that wants to roll through me. Looking at him is like looking at myself before everything changed. He is my exact other half and I fucking hate him for that. People think having an identical twin is the best gift in the world but they are fucking wrong, it's a curse. You look at your twin and see yourself except it's not you, they get to have the happy life while you're dying inside daily.

"I never gave up on you. I looked for you every fucking second of every day." He reaches out and grabs the back of my neck yanking me in until we are leaning our foreheads together. "I. Never. Gave. Up." I hear the truth in his words but I can't accept them. I pull free of his hold and shake my head watching as a curtain of pain falls over his features.

"You didn't try hard enough." He recoils but I push on. "You all carried on living while I prayed for death every fucking day. Want to know what kept me alive, *brother*?" I spit the word at him like it burns my tongue.

"What?" he whispers.

"The thought of you coming for me." A dark chuckle breaks free from me, there is no humor to it. "What a fucking fool, right? The one brother I thought would come for me and it turns out he was too busy burying his cock inside his baby momma." He flinches but I don't stop. "To add insult to injury, a brother did come for me but it wasn't you. It was fucking Gage of all people." He opens his mouth but I'm done, I don't want to hear more of his fucking pathetic lies! I shoulder past him and I don't stop until I reach the threshold of the back door. I peer back at him over my shoulder. "Admit it, all of your lives would have been so much easier if I did die back in Russia." His jaw unhinges at my words. "Do me a favor, stay out of my way and I'll stay out of yours."

Chapter Eight

Clare

Luka and I have yet to say a word to each other. After he carried me out, he placed me in the front seat, buckled me in, then sped out of the Murdoch compound like the car was on fire. I have no idea where he is taking me and honestly, I just don't care. I'm grateful to be away from that place and with my brother. We drive through the city and I stare out the window at the people, they look so carefree and happy with life and that stuns me. Was I just unlucky? Did I do something in a past life to warrant God hating me? I close my eyes and rest my head against the cool glass window. I know God doesn't hate me, it's just easier for me to blame him than face the truth that it's my fault that Tony Murdoch was able to rob me of my child.

"We're here." I blink my eyes open and I'm shocked to

see we're in an underground carpark. Luka gets out and I quickly follow after him. He doesn't slow his pace to let me catch up so I have to jog. He stops when we reach the elevators. I shuffle from foot-to-foot nervously as we wait. I can feel the tension rolling off him in waves, it doesn't ease even as we step into the lift. He pushes 34 and my stomach drops, I'm terrified of heights. The small car is filled with tension so thick you could cut it with a knife, when the doors finally open I sigh in relief and follow after him.

He fishes a key from his back pocket and unlocks the door, holds it open and ushers me inside first. I take three steps before freezing, his house is... beautiful. Dad and I had been living in a double-wide for the past four years while my brother is living in an apartment fit for a wealthy man, white leather couches, stone-top counters, a fake fireplace and windows that span the entirety of the apartment.

"I'm gonna take a shower, make yourself comfortable." I don't even get a chance to reply before he disappears down a small hallway and then I hear a door shut. I make my way cautiously over to the windows, my stomach bottoms out when I see how high up we are. I race back to the couch and drop down. How he can live this high up I'll never know, I would be an anxious mess daily. I don't know how much time passes before Luka makes his way back into the living room, dropping onto the other couch opposite me. Judging from the jeans and Henley he is wearing, he doesn't plan on spending the evening with me and that stings.

"Where are you going?" My throat is sore but I keep the pain from my face. If he doesn't care enough to stay with me and sort through our baggage then I won't give him the satisfaction of seeing me in pain.

"Don't start this shit, Clare." He sounds tired and spent but I don't care.

"What shit? Oh do you mean the shit where you abandon me for a family that isn't even yours?" He pins me with an angry look that dares me to continue, I'm well past carrying that I'll piss him off.

"Watch it," he warns.

"Or what? You'll kick me out? Cut me off?" I say as I throw my hands in the air in frustration.

"You fucking ran from me, Clare!" he shouts, causing me to slink further into the couch as guilt weighs on me.

"I didn't have a choice." I weakly defend, he scoffs and climbs to his feet ready to leave so I follow suit and reach out and grip his arm. He stares down at me and tears begin to build in the back of my eyes. "I'm sorry I hurt you. I swear, Luka, I never meant to make you feel like…"

"Like you and Dad didn't give a fuck about me?" I bite my lip as the first tear falls and nod stiffly. "Fuck!" he rasps out before his arms wrap around me and then smoosh me against his chest as sobs wrack my body. I cling to Luka and allow the tears I refused to let fall when Dad died finally break free. The ugliest sobs tear from deep within my chest as I cry for not just my dad but for the years I lost with my brother, for my baby and for the boy I loved with every fiber of my being. "I got you, Clare-bear," Luka says as he lifts me and carries back to the couch where I curl up on his lap and continue to cry my fucking eyes out. We have a lot of shit to sort out but right now in this moment I am so thankful for my brother. Having his arms around me and making me feel safe, I just know I'll be okay.

I STIR awake to the sound of Luka's voice; he tries to whisper but he's always sucked at that. I smile to myself at the memory then cringe when I open my eyes and feel how puffy and crusty they are from all my tears. I look to the windows and see night has long since fallen, I must have slept for hours which shocks me. Since Dad died, I haven't been sleeping much, mind you. Two weeks after he died the bank repossessed our trailer and I was thrown onto the street without a dime to my name. Pride kept me from reaching out to Luka sooner... well, that and knowing coming back to New York meant I would more than likely run into Rook. I had no idea when I saw on the news that one of the Murdoch brothers was missing that it was Rook. I was only joking around that first day I flew out here, I had no idea he was the missing brother.

"Yeah, I did." I shake my head and focus back on listening in on Luka's conversation. "He strangled my sister, Bish, and I saw red." He releases a loud exhale and nods even though the other person can't see him. "Yeah, I know," he snaps his gaze to me and I see nothing but guilt and shame in his eyes which baffles me. "We'll be there soon." My eyes widen at his admission and I begin to shake my head before he's even ended the call. "I broke protocol today by laying hands on Rook—"

"Luka, no!" I rush to say as I launch off the couch and rush at my brother. I grip the front of his shirt in my hands and cling to him. "Tell them it was me." He cups my face and smiles down at me sadly, I can see he is resigned to whatever fate Bishop Murdoch dishes out and I hate it.

"Go shower and then we'll leave." I shake my head as I step back.

"No, I won't let them hurt you because I kissed Rook." His brow furrows clearly confused. I feel heat creep into my cheeks.

"*You* kissed him?" I bite my lip and nod, embarrassment

engulfs me at having to admit this bit of information to my brother. "What the fuck, Clare?" he shouts, causing me to shrink back a step. "You are not seeing him anymore. I mean it. He isn't a good guy."

I glare at him. "You work for them! How is that any bloody different from me being near Rook?" I don't know why I'm getting so defensive of Rook, he has made his feelings of hatred toward me clear. But, I can see it every time I look into his eyes, the pain and darkness that wants to consume him whole. But I see glimpses of the boy I used to know in there as well. I feel compelled to help him find that little boy again and pull him from the depths of despair.

"Because I know what I'm doing. You on the other hand view the world with rose-colored glasses and that is the type of shit that will get you killed in this world, Clare. You need to stop being fucking naïve and grow up." His words sear me.

"Clearly Rook isn't the only one who has changed a lot in the past four years," I whisper.

"Clare—" I shake my head and wrap my arms around myself.

"Did you know I have been homeless for months since Dad died?" His eyes widen in surprise and he pales slightly. "Did you also know that I am in debt up to my eyeballs trying to pay back all of Dad's medical bills?"

"Why didn't you tell me?" All traces of anger from seconds ago is gone from his tone.

"How could I? I didn't have a phone and plus it's not like you ever called or answered any of my calls when I did have one. I came out here months ago to tell you about Dad and you threw me on the next flight back home to wait for our father to die alone." Tears leak from the corners of my eyes and I'm powerless to stop them. "I busted my ass to pick up shifts at the diner to scrape together enough money to get out here to you and this is the first time we've had a fucking conversation!" I'm screaming at him now and I just don't care. He's my big brother and he wasn't fucking there for me four years ago or five months ago when Dad died. He's never fucking there when I need him the most! He takes a step forward, I take one back not wanting him anywhere near me right now.

"Fuck," he rasps out as he runs a hand through his hair and tugs at the strands in frustration. "We'll finish this conversation when we get back, right now I need you to shower and change. I had some clothes dropped off for you, they're laid out on the bed in the guest room. You'll be staying here with me until my house is ready."

"House?" I query.

He blows out a long exhale before nodding. "Yeah, one of the seven houses near Bishop's is mine." I don't bother to reply to that, my heart aches knowing that he chose the Murdoch's over me, his own family. That is a huge pill to swallow knowing that I'm not enough for my own brother to care about. My last living relative and he would rather be a part of someone else's family than be with me.

Chapter Nine

I sit in his fucking office grinding my teeth. Knight the little snitch bitch went and cried to Bishop about what happened with me and Luka as soon as he walked in the door. Typical fucking Bishop though, he just had his first kid and then transitioned straight into Don mode because Knight is a sulky bitch. Bishop sits behind his desk looking like the true fucking Don that he is. I know he's pissy because Kiara decided to stay at the hospital rather than come home. Car elected to do the same and Vin is just as on edge as Bishop. Vin stands in the corner stiff as fuck and looking worse for wear. It's nearly three in the morning and everyone should be in fucking bed.

"You can't kill him," King says, breaking the tension filled silence. He and Knight occupy the two seats in front of Bishop's desk. Gage and I sit on one of the couches. I don't want to fucking be here but Bishop didn't give me a fucking choice—start falling into line or live here forever. The fucker thinks he can tell me what to do. I almost laugh at the thought. The only reason I am giving into his demands is because me living here means each of them has to see my face daily and I relish in the fact I remind them every single fucking day that they gave up on me, not the other way around.

"What would you have me do? He laid hands on our brother, if I don't punish him then what type of message does it send to the rest of our men?" King bristles in his seat knowing Bish is right. King's just pissed off because his best friend fucked up and is about to pay the price.

"We just——" King clamps his mouth closed at the sound of a knock. Bishop calls out to come in and Luka walks in. What I don't expect is for Clare to trail in after him. He grips her arm and leads her to the couch opposite me. I grit my teeth to keep from lashing out at him for touching her, I have to remind myself she isn't mine to care about. Clare drops into the seat and looks down at her hands in her lap as Luka moves to stand between King and Knight's seat, facing Bishop.

"Care to enlighten me on what the fuck happened earlier?" The cold tone of Bishop's voice lets everyone know he isn't fucking around. Luka may be his most trusted man but that doesn't mean he is exempt from punishment. The little fucker knew this was coming and I'll admit he has bigger balls than I thought. I didn't think he would actually show up but then again I shouldn't be surprised considering who the fuck his step sister is. Clare has always been a firecracker and so innocent. She never used to look so weighed down by life but now it almost seems like life has sucked her dry and spat her back out.

"I have no excuse," Luka says. I give him credit his voice doesn't waiver as he speaks. "I laid hands on Rook and I accept full responsibility for my actions."

"Why did you do it?" Bishop asks as he reclines back in his chair. He may not want to admit it but Bishop is a spitting image of our father in this moment.

"Does it matter?" Luka hedges, Bish quirks a brow at his man.

"Yes," he grits out. "Don't fucking toy with me, Luka, answer the fucking question now because your life depends on your answer." My attention is snagged when Clare rises to her feet and faces Bishop. As if my legs have a mind of their own they follow suit and stand. Bishop looks to her drawing the attention of Luka, King and Knight. Luka goes pale at the sight of her standing there facing off with his boss.

"He did it for me." Silence. That is what her statement is met with. Luka attempts to move toward her but a subtle clearing of King's throat has him pausing. Fucking pussy, he would rather leave her on her own than risk Bishop's wrath. She clears her throat and darts her gaze to me for a second, my breath stills as I wait with bated breath to see if she will air out the truth of what had me snapping.

"Why would something you do cause him a lapse in judgment?" Bish sounds like a condescending bitch and the grunt that comes from Gage tells me he agrees with me.

"B-because it was my fault," she stammers out. "I pushed Rook's boundaries and we got heated then I slipped and hit my head." Surprised as fuck that she didn't rat me out, I'm powerless but to just stand here and stare at her. I can feel Knight's gaze boring into the side of my head. He knows she is lying but he won't tattle because he is too hell bent on trying to get back in my good graces. It's going to take a lot more than him keeping his mouth shut for that to happen.

"You slipped?" Bish queries.

"Y-yes." He purses his lips as he stands, buttons his suit jacket and makes his way around the desk. He perches on the edge closest to King and looks between me, Luka and Clare. The calculating look in his eyes tells me he knows Clare is full of shit, all hope of flying under the radar and letting Luka take the fall just flew fucking out the window.

"Hm, so is this the part Clare where I tell you that room you were in earlier today has cameras in it?" Clare's face turns ashen, she darts her gaze to me. I keep my face blank of all emotion, if Bishop wants to bring this shit up now then he better be ready for the fallout because I'm hyped and ready for all of them to know the fucking truth!

"I-I... it was... I..." Despite my better judgment and wanting to see her suffer I can't. I close the space between us until we are standing shoulder to shoulder and I meet my brother's gaze ignoring everyone else in the room. I don't miss the way she subconsciously shifts closer to me like I'll protect her from my family.

"You really want to do this?" I can hear the bite of my own words. Bishop stands to his full height, King is on his feet and ready to jump in between us if it comes down to that. I see Knight out of the corner of my eye move toward me ready to fight on my behalf, I want to snort at the audacity of his move but don't.

"You really want to stand up against me and question how I run things?" he replies, the both of us stare at each other, daring the other to make the first move in what we both know will further divide me from the rest of them.

"Neither of you need to do this." Bishop and I both ignore Gage and his attempt to ease the situation, we're past the point of no return now.

"You want the truth brother?" I don't bother responding verbally, I just cock a brow egging him on. "You're angry at all of us and blame us all because of what happened to you!" Bishop's composure has slipped, he's yelling now and I fucking love it. It brings me great satisfaction to know I've finally forced him to let his inner thoughts out. "We all fucking tried to find you!"

I smile darkly. I hear King mutter an *oh shit* beneath his breath as I let loose months of pent up hatred. "Was that before or after you were fucking your wife every night, hmm?" I look to King next. "What about you, *brother*? Did you pull your head out of Ally's pussy long enough to even notice I was gone?" An angry storm is brewing in King's green eyes but unlike Bishop's dark brown eyes his hold no malice. Next, I turn to my twin, my other fucking half. He has the good sense to keep his mouth closed and stand tall so we are eye level. "And you, my fucking equal, left me to rot!" My own temper has broken free of its confines and I'm shaking with anger. "None of you cared enough to stop your own fucking lives to worry about me, the only one who cared enough was fucking Gage!"

"I searched for you, every fucking day, you bastard. There was never a second of each day that I didn't think of you." Knight's words may hold truth to them but they mean nothing to me.

"Aww, poor you." His eyes narrow to angry slits. "That must have been so hard for *you*, worrying every day that you got to sleep in your own bed, shove your cock inside Koby each night while Ivan shoved his in my fucking ass every fucking day!" I scream so fucking loud, everyone in the room gasps. Knight stumbles back a step with a horrified look on his face.

"Rook—" I spin back toward Bishop and pin him with a look that has him clamping his mouth closed. Satisfied that I shut him down I turn to face Gage, he stiffens but says nothing as he waits for me to unleash my fury on him.

"You know when Vlad handed Anya over to Ivan I was there." The look of surprise that colors his features tells me Anya left that part out. "Your girl got a front row seat to the action, she saw what I was willing to do just so he wouldn't torture me anymore." I grip the hem of my shirt and yank it over my head, I hear their sharp intakes of breath as they take in the scars that litter my body. My skin used to be smooth and something to admire but now, it is littered with cigarette burns, slashes from blades, bullet wounds and so many other things. "Take a good look at me, brothers. This could have been any one of you lucky sons of bitches," I taunt. Because I'm a sadistic mother fucker I turn to Clare. I'll admit I'm shocked to find her gaze on mine and not the scars that mark my body. "Still think I'm pretty, *Pyro?*" My old pet name for her rolls off my tongue with ease and has her breath hitching at hearing it. "You still want to kiss me now?" I don't give her a chance to answer. "Would you let a monster like me beneath your sheets again?"

"Rook, that's enough!" King tries to cut in but Clare answers the same time as he speaks

"Yes." That one word stumps me.

"Why?" I bite out, her features soften as she reaches out to touch me. I tense and she drops her hand back to her side.

"You have scars that tell a story but they aren't how your story will end, Rook."

"You don't know shit!" I grit out through clenched teeth.

"You may be right but I also know that you're full of shit." I hear Gage and King mutter beneath their breath but I ignore them as I focus on the girl that ruined me before Ivan could have. Clare has no idea that she held more power over me then Ivan ever did in the eight months I was with him. She is the only person who was able to simultaneously destroy me both mentally and emotionally. "Your trying to push everyone away because you feel like you deserve to be shrouded in the darkness you allow yourself to live in. Don't let your demons win, Rook, because you're better than that."

This woman has no fucking idea what she is saying. I don't choose this! I'm stuck in this rut because of that Russian cunt. He starved me, tore chunks of hair from my head, beat me daily, raped me and forced me to do things I never would have dreamed of doing. It's a struggle every fucking day for me to get my ass out of bed and train. I'm trying to gain back the muscle I lost from being chained like a *mutt*. A shudder rolls through at the thought of that word, my name *Dvornyaga* (*mutt*) is what he used to call me.

"You don't know shit about me. Don't fucking stand here and think you have any right to speak to me after what you did!" She recoils at the anger in my tone, good. Clare is a nuisance that I thought I had got rid of years ago but like all cockroaches, she came crawling back.

Chapter Ten

Clare

One week later...

Luka left early this morning to catch his flight to Russia with Gage and Anya. He is going to be traveling a lot since Bishop has declared he needs to be home with Kiara and their son—Royal. Rook's sister's little girl—Channel is stunning as well. Kiara and Carlina have been texting me and checking in which is odd considering we barely know each other but, both these girls are amazing and so kind. Koby and Anya aren't mean or anything but I can tell they are on edge when I am around just waiting for Rook to finally snap. Allison, I have learnt is the mothering type. She texts me but not as much as the other two because she is studying to be a nurse and homeschooling her daughter.

Ally is the one who actually helped me get my job at the local animal shelter. I freaking love working there! Luka and I had a chat about me needing to get my own place, honestly it was like getting sucker punched but I also know that he needs his space back. Having his little sister live with him isn't ideal for picking up the ladies. My problem though, I cannot afford to live in the city. I don't even make enough to cover a month's worth of rent. I don't know what's up with Luka but he isn't the same as he once was. I know he's still angry with me because I won't tell him how I know Rook or why there is so much bad blood between us. Truth is, I can't tell him the reason why Rook and I can't stomach being in the same room together when I can't even tell Rook the truth.

A loud knock on the door pulls me from my thoughts, not knowing who the heck it could be ,I decide to peek through the peephole and gasp. I quickly undo the chain and unlock the door before opening it, there he stands looking effortlessly gorgeous. Black jeans, a white tee and a varsity jacket that's opened. His hair is spiked and his face is clean shaven which tells me in the time since I last saw him something has changed. His eyes don't seem to spit fire at me either.

"You gonna invite me in?" His voice is like a balm to my battered soul but I also can't allow him to lull me into a false sense of hope. He has so many anger issues to work through and I refuse to be his punching bag, I've been through enough.

"You gonna yell at me if I do?" He rolls his eyes and shoves his hands in his pockets as he rocks back on his heels. I blow out an exasperated breath and step aside allowing him entry. He makes sure to keep enough space between our bodies as he enters, it's physical contact that is a trigger for him. I close the door and follow after him. Judging from how he knows where to go and doesn't bother to look around, he's been here before. He drops into one of Luka's white leather single chairs in the living room, eyeing me. Too wired to sit, I perch on the arm of the sofa and try not to fidget.

"Are you staying or you planning on leaving again?" A whoosh of air escapes me at his blatant jab, maybe I need to just come clean and hope that we can move past... this hatred. Well, hatred on his part. I don't hate Rook, how could you hate someone you're still in love with?

"If you're asking if I plan on staying in New York? Then yes, I don't plan on going back to Oklahoma," I answer honestly. He purses his lips and runs his gaze over me causing me to grow warm under the pressure of his stare.

"Not gonna miss your friends or *boyfriend?*" I narrow my eyes and shake my head.

"If you've just come here to throw more insults around and accuse me of being a whore, you can just leave," I snap.

"So that's a no to the boyfriend then." His sarcastic tone just pisses me off.

"No, there is no boyfriend. The only person that has even come close to wearing that title currently sits across from me glaring daggers my way. Happy now?" If I wasn't paying such close attention I would have missed his eyes widening slightly at my declaration before he quickly masks his features. "Why are you here when you have made it clear you hate me and I'm not welcome around you?"

"You fucking ruined us!" he shouts. His outburst shocks the hell out of me that I don't even realize I've leapt off the arm of the sofa until he closes the space between us and scowls down at me.

"I-I didn't do anything," I weakly protest. His eyes

darken further, the anger I thought had lessened earlier has returned tenfold.

"You dirty little liar. You turn up at my house, tell me you're pregnant and then three days later disappear without a fucking trace except for a fucking letter!" I stumble back a step and shake my head denying his claim.

"I never left you a letter."

"Bullshit!" He reaches into his back pocket and pulls out a crumpled piece of paper and holds it out to me. I tentatively reach out and grab it with shaky fingers. Unfolding the paper I can already tell it isn't my writing, taking a deep breath I read the letter.

> Rook,
> By the time you read this I'll already be hundreds of miles away. Don't try to find me.
> I dealt with the problem, you don't have to worry anymore I took care of it. Whatever this was between us is over, you're no good for me.
> Clare.

I grit my teeth and squash the paper in my fist as I stare up at him vibrating with rage. "How the fuck could you have thought *I* wrote that stupid ass letter?" I don't give him a chance to answer. "You really think I would have called our child an *it?* You clearly didn't know me as well as I thought you did if you believe this bullshit!" I scream as I throw the ball of paper at him and storm out of the room. I can't stomach the sight of him right now! I hear his footsteps chase after me but I don't stop until I reach my room. I'm tempted to slam the door but I know Rook and a door won't stop him from getting to me. I keep my back to him as I ruffle through my bag to find some clothes to wear to work.

"Don't fucking walk away from me!" he shouts. I continue to ignore him as I pull out some jeans and a long-sleeve shirt I snagged from the clearance section at Target. I don't have an ensuite in my room like Luka does, so I turn and pin him with a look that I hope reads *get the hell out.*

"You can leave now. I have somewhere to be." The words have just left my mouth when he eats up the distance between us, wraps his hand around my throat and slams me back against the wall. I should be terrified at the position I'm in but I'm not. Rook can talk a big game and claim he hates me but the truth is, I know him. Rook would never hurt me, his body and words say one thing but his eyes give him away. I see the longing and love in them even when he thinks he's masked his emotions perfectly.

"Where the fuck do you think you're going?" he growls right in my face.

"Unlike you, some of us actually have to work for a living so we can keep a roof over our heads." His brows furrow and I can see the confusion in his eyes.

"What?" I roll my eyes and fight the urge to shove him back. I know he wouldn't willingly hurt me but I also know that from the last time I touched him that physical contact triggers him and this time I don't think anyone will be coming to my rescue.

"I have a job. Which I will be late for if you don't unhand me and back up." For three seconds he stands there unmoving and unblinking so I decide to throw caution out the window and reach up to grip the hand that is currently locked around my throat. I hold his gaze the entire time as I grip his hand and pull it away. His eyes track my movements almost like he is shocked my touch hasn't set him on fire. Deciding to push my luck further I interlock our fingers and reach up with my free hand to cup his cheek bringing his gaze back to me. The vulnerability in his eyes sears me, I hate that look and never want to see it on him again. "I'm so sorry."

He darts his tongue out to moisten his lips and like a moth to a flame I track each of his movements. Flashes of memories play on a reel in my mind of what that tongue tastes like and what he can do with it. I can only imagine how much better he is at using it now after years of experience.

"I wish that was enough," he whispers as he steps back, causing my arms to drop back to my sides. I sigh and nod, knowing that he isn't ready to hear the truth from me. I brush past him and decide that if he isn't going to give me privacy, I'll change right here with him in the room. I keep my back to him as I grip the hem of my shirt and pull it over my head. His sharp intake of breath has me feeling emboldened. I pop the button on my shorts next and push them down my legs. I'm so thankful I decided to wear my black lace panties and a matching black bra rather than my normal cotton ones. I grab my jeans off the bed and shimmy into them. Just as I reach for my shirt, I'm spun around and shoved onto the bed. Rook looms above me with a heated look in his eyes but I can also see uncertainty in his gaze.

"You... I don't want you," he says out loud but more to himself so I don't answer. "I hate you for what you did but... I can't fucking stay away from you." I push up from the bed and stand, he's close that our chests touch. I crane my neck to meet his hooded gaze. My breaths are coming in fast pants, my body is buzzing with awareness at how close he is to me. I open my mouth to speak but the words die on my tongue when he bends down and smashes his lips against mine. I gasp into his mouth, his tongue plunges inside my mouth and I moan at the taste of him. I reach out and grip the lapels of his jacket, that move seems to snap him out of the moment and he yanks back so fast he stumbles until he smacks against the wall.

We both stand here staring at each other in shock at what just happened. His chest is rising and falling in quick succession. I see the fight or flight cross his features, I don't know what possesses me to blurt the words but I do.

"Don't go." I blindly reach behind me for my shirt as I quickly yank it on and stare at him only to see he hasn't moved an inch. "Come to work with me and then maybe we can just... hang out after?" No words are exchanged for a minute. I didn't realize I was holding my breath until the air rushes out of me when he nods curtly and excitement at the prospect of spending the afternoon with Rook thrums through me.

Chapter Eleven

I've been following her around this place for hours watching as she plays with all the animals. I get her love for cats and dogs but the fucking birds and reptiles I don't fucking understand! The girl has no fucking fear. She just picked a snake up like it was nothing as Amber–the manager–grabbed a clutch of snake eggs out from under it. I've barely said two words to her since the kiss, I don't know what the fuck to say. The truth is I'm fucking shocked I managed to not black out and hurt her like last time, I even got hard at seeing her in that lace set. I haven't gotten hard since... since I was in Russia. I text Opal on our way here and told her I needed to see her tomorrow. She was quick to agree.

Clare's words from the other night have been on repeat

in my mind. Am I choosing to wallow in this darkness? I want to say no but then another part of me, a small part keeps whispering that I am and I hate that voice for causing me to doubt myself. I've even hung out with Koby and the twins a lot in the past week when Knight isn't around. Shit, I even hung out with Kiara and Car and met my new nephew and niece. I don't know why I can stand to be around the girls but throw my brother's in the mix and I'm out. I mean, I can stomach being around Gage but the other three, nah. I'm so angry and bitter toward them. Car and I make small talk but the truth is, I don't really know my sister anymore. She has changed so much—she's a wife and mother now. She's not my Car anymore, she's Vin's.

"Rook?" I shake my head to clear my thoughts and turn to look at Clare who in some weird pen cage looking thing kneeling down and playing with a... is it a fucking rat?

"What the hell is that?" I can hear the horror in my own voice, she rolls her eyes and smiles down at the *thing*.

"Don't listen to the mean man *Bob*, you're beautiful." I scrunch my face up.

"It's name is Bob?" She glares playfully up at me as she scoops the thing into her arms and stands, coming closer, causing me to back up a step.

"Bob is a Yorkshire terrier and the runt of his litter. His mother didn't want him so she refused to feed him. He's eight weeks old and isn't he so cute?" She has to be out her fucking mind. This black, blue and white multi colored dog is not fucking cute, it looks like a hairy fucking rat!

"It looks like a–" She pins me with a warning look that has me clamping my mouth closed and fighting not to laugh. Just the notion of me wanting to laugh has my mood spiraling. Whenever I'm around her, I've noticed that I forget everything and how I'm feeling. Which is why I turn and leave, ignoring her calls for me to come back.

I SIT HERE STARING at Opal waiting for her to digest everything I told her about what happened between me and Clare yesterday. I ignored all her calls and texts, unable to speak to her. I did come home to Bishop telling me that Luka would be in Russia for two weeks, then he's being sent to Miami to check in with Tony after that as part of his punishment. Luka may be pissed he's been sent away but as opposed to a bullet in the head, he took this punishment on the chin. I'm not mad that he'll be out of the country because that means Clare will be at my mercy.

"How did that make you feel, kissing Clare?" I focus back on the here and now as I answer Opal.

"I didn't think," I answer honestly.

"Care to explain?" I roll my lips over my teeth debating if I should tell her or not. It's at that second Clare's words infiltrate my mind and makes the decision for me.

"Being with Clare is like second nature. I didn't think when I kissed her yesterday, it just happened and it was like my mind... was quiet." She hums and nods which has me wondering what the fuck she is thinking.

"Without you or Clare knowing it, she is helping you heal." I scrunch my face causing her to smile as she continues, "Hear me out. Since Clare has come into your life, you no longer hide out in your room. You are speaking with your sister-in-laws and spending time with your nieces and nephews now. You even left the house on your own yesterday! That is a huge step, Rook." I mull over her words and let them sink in for a minute. I never gave it a second thought when I left yesterday to go see Clare, I just knew I had to see her.

"I don't trust her." Opal's features pull taut as she nods, as if she understands my situation.

"I understand, Rook. Trust will come with time. Believe me when I say you are lucky to have a family that cares and a person like Clare who is willing to help you."

"Why do you say that?" Talking to Opal seems to come easily to me today. She doesn't seem shocked though, she just seems like she expected me to eventually open up.

"Because I never had any of that when Tony Bennett rescued me." I cock my head to the side confused.

"Tony did what?" She smiles shyly as she answers.

"All I will say is that I was trafficked as a child. My family sold me and I was raped by more men than you can count. I thought death would be my only option until Tony gave me a chance at a life different from the only one I knew. I grabbed it with both hands and swore I would never allow the scars of my past to taint my bright future." I fall further back into the couch and look at Opal in a whole new light, she doesn't look jaded or bitter.

"How are you so..." I can't find the right word but Opal takes pity on me and helps me out.

"Happy? Resilient?" I nod. "Because happiness is a choice, Rook. I would choose to be happy every day rather than lay in bed and relive the horrors of my past. If I did that, I would never get up and be able to do what I do. I went through hell, but because of what I went through I am able to sit here and help others and *really* understand their situation." Something inside me clicks and I wind up telling her everything. We sit here for nearly four hours and not once does she ever check her watch or the clock on the wall. She makes me feel heard and understood. I had no idea how freeing it would feel to tell someone about what I went through.

"I can be near the girls and the kids but not my brothers. I'm so fucking angry at them. Even being near Clare fucks with my head. I look at her and I feel... something other than disgust at the thought of sex but I also want to strangle her."

"Okay, about your brothers. I think it would be a good idea, but only when *you* are ready, to have them join us for a session and explain to them how you really feel." I don't protest because a part of me knows in order for me to really heal and get over this hatred and anger I feel toward them, I have to face it head on. "Now, with Clare, it is a good thing that she makes you feel something. Just remember, Rook, everything is at your pace not hers, your brothers or anyone else's. What you went through is going to take time and a lot of healing to live with because you will never forget it, but you will learn ways to live with it daily."

"That's all I want. I just don't want to feel like I'm suffocating every day that I wake up. I'm not ready for the talk with my brothers. I'm still so fucking mad at them for leaving me behind and moving on with their lives." I can hear the anger in my own voice.

"You have every right to feel how you do, your feelings are valid, Rook. By the sounds of things, it would be easier for you to deal with things with Clare before your brothers. Am I right to assume that?" I think about that for a minute before I reluctantly nod. "Have you thought about just spending time with Clare? There doesn't need to be anything physical or sexual, maybe you could watch a movie?"

I shake my head. "That's the thing, when I'm with her I want to touch her but I don't know how without blacking out again. I saw her practically naked and my cock was rock fucking hard at the sight of her, what the fuck is wrong with me?" I drop my chin to my chest, emotionally fucking spent from talking for hours.

"Nothing is wrong with you. Sex isn't something that is disgusting, Rook. It is something to be shared with someone you care about and it can be a beautiful thing." I meet her stare with a hard look.

"That's the thing. Sex has only ever been enjoyable when it was Clare. Every other girl after her meant nothing to me, they were just some nameless, faceless hole to take the edge off while I was picturing Clare's face every time I came." Opal nods her understanding.

"Only you will know when the time is right for you to take that next step with Clare."

"But what if I hurt her again? Don't get me wrong, I may still be fucking angry at her but I don't actually want to cause her physical harm." Shame washes over me at the thought of how I strangled her. If Knight didn't come in when he did, I would have killed her.

"You tell her, you make sure she knows how you feel and let her know that you need her to keep you present. The first time you do have sex it is going to be hard, there may be flashbacks that could trigger your rage or you could wind up in a corner. Everyone is different but I want you to know I am available to you, day and night if you should need me." I smile my thanks and for the first time I don't actually have to force it.

"So, any chance you can tell Bishop to give me the keys to my house now?" I push, her eyes shine with mirth.

"Yeah. I think you're ready for the next step in your healing, so I'll tell him my thoughts."

Rook - 1

Bishop – 0

Stick that in your peace pipe and smoke it, asshole. I walk out of my session with Opal feeling fucking lighter than I have in months and shockingly, I'm actually smiling. Now, I just need to call the shelter and set my plan in motion for the green-eyed monster that is no doubt pissed as fuck at me.

Chapter Twelve

Clare

I'm sitting here at the counter in the kitchen working out a payment plan for dad's medical bills when the intercom sounds. I march over to where the phone hangs in its cradle by the front door and hesitantly pick it up.

"Hello?" I ask.

"Miss Santiago, this is Meg from reception."

"Uh, okay?"

"Mr. Salinski let us know he was away and if we had any deliveries to contact you." Relief washes over me, Luka must have a parcel down stairs.

"Yeah, of course I can come down and collect the package for my brother now."

"Oh, thank you but the package is addressed to you Miss Santiago." Shocked and confused as to who the hell sent me something, I tell Meg I'm on my way. I snag my keys and lock the door behind myself as I head down to reception to help them sort out this mix up because there is no way someone sent me something—I don't have anyone who cares enough to send me shit. I tap my foot anxiously as I wait for the elevator to hit the lobby. It still baffles me how my brother who grew up modestly like me can live in such a lavish place like this. When the car finally comes to a stop and the doors open, I sigh in relief as I head for the reception desk. A blonde woman beams at me when she sees me approaching, her name tag reads Meg so I smile kindly as I come to a stop.

"Hi, I'm Clare?" I don't know why I voiced it as a question and mentally facepalm myself.

"I am so jealous. He is just the sweetest little thing." I cock my head to the side and screw my face up thoroughly confused at what she is meaning.

"I don't—" The words die in my throat when she bends down to retrieve something, when she places the little cage on the desk my eyes widen and I gasp. "Bob?" I keep darting my gaze between the little Yorkshire terrier and the woman behind the desk. "He—I mean, I don't... he can't..." I can't string a coherent sentence together. As if my hands have a mind of their own, they reach out and open the cage door. Bob whimpers before leaping into my arms. I hold him close to my chest and nuzzle his head.

"There is a note, Miss Santiago." I cut a glance to Meg to see a cream colored envelope in her hand. I settle Bob into my side as I thank her and grab the letter. I tear it open feeling Meg's gaze on me the entire time.

Your phone must be broken!

You blew mine up non-stop and when I return the favor your phone suddenly doesn't ring and my messages bounce back! I can't help the chuckle that breaks free.

So, to say I'm sorry for being a dick I sent you a gift which I think at least warrants a thank you call.

P.S. I still think it looks like a fucking rat!

Beaming from ear to ear, I snag Bob's crate, thank Meg and rush back to the elevators. The ride back up seems to take longer than getting down. As soon as the doors open, I race back to Luka's and manage not to drop Bob or the crate as I unlock and open the door. I drop the crate by the living room and race to my room to grab my phone. I unlock it and quickly scroll through my settings to unblock Rook and hit dial. My stomach is in knots as I wait for him to answer. The longer it rings, my hope begins to dwindle that he'll answer.

"Pyro." I smile so wide it hurts at hearing his voice and my old nickname.

"You got me Bob!" I screech. I hear him muttering something to someone before a door closes and then his voice fills the line again.

"Your boss was excited as fuck to wrap the thing up and send it to you." I purse my lips.

"He is not a thing! Bob is just a baby. I'm so thankful you were sweet enough to get him for me, Rook, but..." I close my eyes not wanting to see the look on Bob's face as I say what I do next. "I can't afford a dog, Rook," I whisper and pray I don't piss him off.

"Why the fuck not?" he snaps.

"Because I can't. I'm with Luka and I can't afford a place in the city, let alone food for a dog–" Knocking at the front door has me pausing and rushing out of my room to answer it. I assume it's Meg and I forgot to sign for the package, so I don't check the peephole. I just swing the door open and stare like an idiot. Rook reaches out to grab my phone from my hand and ends our call as he brushes past me. I don't miss the fact that he didn't jump away from me when he brushed up against me. I snap out of my stupor and push the door closed then chase after Rook. I find him in the living room gazing out the windows. "Rook, what are you doing here?" He slowly turns to face me with an unreadable look on his face.

"I was in the lobby, I saw your face when you realized that the *rat*—" I pin him with a scathing look that has him backtracking. "The dog was yours. I'm not letting you give it up." I look down at Bob who is now nestled against my chest and sleeping soundly. I gently pat his little face and smile before turning my attention back to the man who just bought me my first ever pet.

"Don't get me wrong, I am so thankful you got him for me and honestly I love that you did it but I can't afford to keep him."

"Why the fuck not?" I pin him with a look that I hope conveys my frustrations.

"I have to pay rent, food, utilities as well as my father's medical bills. Out of those four things I can only afford two so I guess I'll have no food or hot water," I say with a shrug. His eyes darken as his upper lips pulls back in a snarl that has me confused as hell.

"Why the fuck isn't your *brother* helping you?" All the air rushes out of me and I drop my gaze to the floor, too ashamed to hold his gaze as I answer.

"I don't know. I think he's still angry Dad and I left without a trace." Rook snorts.

"Yeah I know the feeling but here I fucking am still trying to help you when I should run for the fucking hills." I slowly lift my gaze back to his, dart my tongue out to wet my lips and relish in the way his eyes track my every move.

"Why don't you run? You don't owe me anything, Rook. I don't expect you to take pity on me because—"

"I would never do anything for you out of pity, Clare. I'd do it because of who you are to me." Feeling emboldened I push him.

"Who am I to you?" His eyes darken, he eats the space up between us until we are nearly chest to chest. The tension between us ramps up, I can feel the heat of his body like a whispered caress brushing over my skin. It takes more strength than I want to admit not to press against him.

"My past." He reaches out to cup the back of my neck. "My present." He cups my cheek with his other hand. "My future," he whispers as he places the softest kiss against my lips. It's over too fast. He pulls back and gazes down at me. "I'm still so furious with you, Clare, and mark my words, we are going to talk this shit out one day but right now, I need you with me."

"Why?" I ask thoroughly confused.

"Because neither of us knew it, but you just being around me is helping me in more ways than I care to admit." I shake my head denying his claim.

"Rook, we can't even spend a whole day together without fighting. How is *that* helping you?" I can see the torment in his eyes, he wants to lie but he won't.

"I don't fucking know, Clare. All I know is you make me want to try and not be stuck in this fucking rut. So, you can either stay here with your asshole brother and live on struggle street or—"

"Or what?" I cut in. He steps back and holds his arms out wide with a panty-melting smirk on his luscious lips.

"You can be my new roommate and I promise you can afford this rent." I narrow my eyes.

"What's the price?" I ask hesitantly.

"It's not riding my dick if that's what you're thinking?" I fake gasp, but the truth is, that is exactly what I was *hoping* the price would be.

"I-I wasn't," I weakly protest, which only causes him to smile.

"I'll pretend that I believe you." I roll my eyes and head into the kitchen to grab a bowl to fill with some water for Bob. Rook follows after me and watches silently as I set the bowl and Bob down. "If you come live with me, I'll pay for everything for the dog." I flick my gaze to him and I'll admit I'm shocked to see that he is serious.

"*If* I agree, I want to pay my way. I'm no mooch, Rook. I just want to pay my dad's debt then study to become a vet nurse."

"Girl, quit acting like you're gonna pass this opportunity up and pack your shit," he says, followed by the melodic sound of his laughter that has butterflies taking flight inside me.

Chapter Thirteen

Rook

One week later...

Sitting here across from Clare, watching as she eats her Pad Thai has a feeling of longing hitting me square in the chest. Bishop gave us all the keys to our houses the morning I went to Clare's to give her Bob, then she and I both moved into my house that night and haven't looked back since. She stays in the room opposite mine. Each morning we wake up and have breakfast together, then I drive her to work before returning to meet with Opal. Opal thinks Clare being here is helping me heal and recover. I don't deny it because I know it's true.

Seven days together and I find myself excited to wake up and see what the day will bring. Each night Clare and I cook dinner together. She refuses to waste money on takeout and truth is, I attempt to cook and burn it, then Clare takes pity on me and cooks us both dinner. All I seem to be able to manage to cook is bacon and fucking eggs. Other than that, I'm fucked. The sound of Clare's phone ringing draws my attention back to the present. She checks the caller ID and her face drops.

"Who is it?" I ask. She takes a deep inhale of breath before meeting my stare.

"No one," she lies, and it grates on my fucking nerves.

"Either you answer me truthfully or I get Vin or Knight to hack your phone records and call the number back myself," I warn. Her eyes widen for a second before she winds up scowling at me.

"It's the people chasing the money for Dad's medical bills. Happy now?" she snaps as she stands and dumps her plate in the sink before storming out of the room with Bob hot on her heels. I glare at the fucking hairy rat. The little fucker has pissed everywhere while she is at work. It's like the monster knows to fuck with me while she is gone. I left the front door open the other day hoping he would run outside, then I could lie and say someone stole him or some shit. The bastard sat at the front door with an evil look in its eyes before racing off to Clare's room. I give her fifteen minutes of time alone before I'm racing up the stairs after her. I don't bother to knock as I push her door open and glare at the fucking rat on her bed as he barks at me.

"Get out!" I dart my gaze to the adjoining bathroom to see her standing there in nothing but a white towel. Her hair is wet and I watch as droplets of water drip down her chest. I can feel my cock growing hard at the sight of her. This time I don't panic when I feel my length growing hard, thoughts of burying my cock inside her is what snaps me from my stunned state. "Rook?"

I shake my head and drag my eyes back to hers. I hate to admit it but it takes more force than I want to admit. "Yeah?"

She rolls her eyes clearly exasperated by my presence. "Why are you in my room?" Uh, that is a good question, one that I can't answer because seeing her practically naked has wiped my train of thought.

"I... You and I we uh, we need to—"

"Talk?" she supplies, and like an idiot I nod. "Well can you give me like five minutes to change and then I'll meet you downstairs?" Again, I nod. As I turn to leave, the fucking rat growls at me. I pin the bastard with a glare as I say,

"The rat stays here!" Her shocked gasp follows me out of the room. It may sound crazy but I puff my chest a little knowing that I just one upped the rat.

I WAIT in the living room, in front of the open fire, for Clare. I give Bishop that, he really did do well with designing these houses. I would *never* tell the asshole that though. The whole lower level of my house has majority windows instead of walls. I like that because I don't feel enclosed. Since my time in Russia, I hate being closed in, so knowing I can see out wherever I look has my anxiety easing. I have only discovered this week that I have PTSD and anxiety, which shouldn't shock me but it does. Opal says that over time I will learn how to manage it. I drop onto the brown leather sofa and kick my feet up on the coffee table in front of me. I gaze out the window in front of me and smile, the night sky is lit up by stars.

I pull my phone from my pocket and scroll through my contacts until I find Vin's number. I hit call and wait for him to answer.

"Rook?" he answers on the third ring.

"Yeah." Silence ensues as we both sit here awkwardly waiting for the other to speak. I don't know him really, so me calling him out of the blue must be as weird for him as it is for me.

"Is everything... okay?" A whoosh of air escapes me before I launch into asking him for a favor. He doesn't hesitate to agree to help me and for that I am beyond fucking grateful. He and Car live in the house opposite mine, King is to their left and Gage to their right. Knight's house is on my right and the house on my left is empty. It was supposed to go to Luka but I put my foot down and said no. Bishop agreed without argument. Luka can eat a bag of assholes for all I care. I don't know what his deal is, but leaving Clare high and dry like he has, it's really pissed me off. I end the call with Vin just as Clare saunters into the room. I like seeing her in the new clothes I bought her. She threw a fit about me spending money on her and that she isn't a charity case but the truth is, she busts her ass daily at her job and doesn't make enough to cover shit. I just wanted to do something nice for her. Once she cooled off, she thanked me and admitted that she hadn't had new clothes in years. That pissed me off. I also just learned that she was her father's primary caregiver while her *brother* was here playing happy families with mine.

"You wanted to see me?" she asks as she drops down next to me. Mere days ago I would have launched away from her being this close but now, I crave her nearness. I love feeling her skin against mine and if the shivers that roll through her when I brush up against her are any signs to go by, she loves me touching her as well. I gaze down at her and hate that I can see blind trust in her gaze. She has no idea that I want to watch the life drain from her eyes while making sure no harm ever comes to her.

"Why did you do it?" I whisper. She doesn't pretend to not know what I am asking. Her shoulders hunch forward and she drops her chin to her chest as she starts to fiddle with her fingers in her lap. "Answer me," I push. She slowly turns her face to look up at me and I see tears brimming her eyes.

"I didn't have a choice," she says so low that I would have missed it if I wasn't paying such close attention. Anger rushes through me at her answer. I stand and glare down my nose at her. She looks so tiny and broken sitting there but I don't give a shit! I need to hear her reasoning behind why she ran and killed my fucking kid!

"That isn't a fucking answer!" I shout. She flinches but I'm past the point of caring now. We have danced around the elephant in the room since she moved in, and it is high fucking time we addressed this issue! "Why the hell did you run from me and kill my fucking kid? You said you wanted the baby with *me*. I was ready to give you everything instead you broke my fucking heart!" I scream the last bit. Tears flow freely down her cheeks as she grips the hem of her shirt in a vice like grip. She climbs to her feet and yanks her shirt over her head, I glare at the little witch. "Trying to seduce me isn't going to work. I'm fucking damaged, remember?" She pins me with a look that would have a lesser man trembling and backing down.

Chapter Fourteen

I stand here in front of the boy who I have loved since I was fifteen and hate that I see hatred in his gaze, when all I feel for him is love. If I tell him the truth about what happened to our baby, it is going to rock him to the core. I haven't said anything out of fear of pushing him further into the dark abyss he has been hiding in. We may talk every day but never about him and what he went through at the hands of his brother's enemy. I'll admit I am green with envy that he sees and speaks to Opal every day. I know that is petty and such schoolgirl bullshit, but it's how I feel.

"Put your fucking clothes on and stop acting like a hussy!" His words brand me with anger.

"The only person I have ever been a *hussy* for is you!

Unlike you, I didn't get butt hurt and fuck my way through the cheer squad at my nice private school."

"Nah, you just run away and murder babies." Anger like I have never felt before courses through my veins. I don't care if I trigger him, so I shove him backward and relish at the shocked look on his face. I pop the button on my jeans and peel the left side down so he can see the scar that his father left behind.

"You see that?" I don't give him a chance to answer as I push on. "Your daddy found out about our *bastard* as he put it and Tony-fucking-Murdoch made sure that I never had an option of if *my* fucking baby lived! For years you have sat atop your high horse and looked down your nose at me. The truth is your father hunted me down like a dog and stabbed me, then he and another one of his men took turns beating my ass to make sure the baby was well and truly dead. There you go, baby Murdoch, that's the truth." Rook is pale and looks like he has seen a ghost but I don't care. I fight past the lump in my throat and brush away the tears as I continue. "The next time you stand there and say I killed *my* baby, I will gut you like a fucking pig! I ran from you because Tony said he wouldn't kill me but he would kill you if I stayed!" I don't wait around for his reply, I run from the living room and race up the stairs to the safety of my room.

I'VE BEEN CURLED up on my bed for over an hour crying with Bob clutched against my chest. Bob has been licking my tears and trying his best to comfort me. Unfortunately for him, the one person who I want to comfort me right now is the person who put me in this state. I never wanted to explode at him the way I did but the truth is, it was like a veil came over me and an ugly monster took control. I bury my face in the pillow to try to muffle the sounds of my sobs. I've heard him come upstairs a couple times and pace outside my room before retreating back down the stairs. I hate that I don't work tomorrow and will be stuck at home with him all day. That's fine though, I plan on staying in my room all day and avoiding him like he is Covid-19!

I'm roused awake by the feeling of the bed dipping. I slowly blink my eyes open and swallow back the scream that wants to break free when I see a figure on the side of my bed. I know without even having to see him that it's Rook. It's crazy, but it's like my body always knows when he is near. I want to fake that I'm still asleep but I also know that him coming in here must have taken a lot of effort on his part. So, I shuffle back and rest against the headboard, trying not to disturb Bob who sleeps soundly on the other side of the bed. I reach for the bedside lamp but his words stop me.

"Leave it... please." I only listen because he said *please*. I can make out the outline of him in the darkness and even when I'm so angry with him, I hate that my heart still aches with the need to wipe away his worries and fears. "The night I took Koby to the docks..." the air lodges in my lungs, he's about to tell me his story! "It was only to scare her. I just wanted her to admit that she was a plant and playing my brother. Knight and I may be identical but we are polar opposites. He hid in the shadows while I danced in the limelight and buried my pain beneath humor and jokes. Knight was coming out of the darkness and I hated that it was because of a girl and not... *me*."

I remain silent not wanting to ask why in case he stops talking. I want–no—need to hear his story. "I pretended to be Knight when I picked her up. No one can tell us apart, aside from our family and now the girls. She knocked me on my ass when she figured it out quicker than I thought she would. As soon as I pulled up to the docks, I knew something wasn't right. I could just feel it, ya know?" I nod my head agreeing with him, not sure if he can even see my reaction. "We got pinned down when the Russian's spotted us. It was in that moment when they fired round after round at us that I knew Koby was telling the truth." He begins to clam up so I take a risk and reach out to grab one of his hands and hold it in mine, offering my support.

"If this is too much, you don't have to tell me, Rook." He squeezes my hand and I see him shake his head in the darkness.

"I need to tell... *you*. Opal knows some of it but not all. I can't go to my brothers or the girls with any of this so, please, just—"

"I'll listen to everything you have to say but just know, no matter what you tell me, I'll still be here and not look at you any different, I swear." My words seem to reassure him enough for him to continue.

"I didn't hesitate when Ivan called out to Koby. I knew it would kill Knight if something happened to her, so I took the shots for her. I expected to die that night on the docks and sometimes I wish I did." I gasp hating that he feels this way. "I don't remember what happened after the explosion went off. All I recall is waking up in some room, strapped to a bed with IV lines poking out of me and hearing a constant beeping sound. The Russian's saved me but they didn't do it because they cared. Ivan made sure I had the best surgeons but I was never given any pain relief after the surgery. The pain was excruciating My dumb ass thought that would be the worst of it, how fucking wrong was I."

I can hear the bitterness that coats his words but I can also hear the hatred in his tone. It just shocks the hell out of me when I realize the hatred is directed at himself and not the monster that hurt him!

"While I was strapped to the bed, writhing in pain, Ivan started his... game. He said *I don't want you to get bored, so, I'm here to keep you* happy! I wish I never found out what his version of happiness was." The anguish in his voice spears me right in the heart. I can feel myself growing tense as I wait for the worst of the story. "I couldn't move—my hands, feet, torso and thighs were strapped to a make-shift hospital bed. It started out with him just running his hands along my arms and legs then... t-then he moved onto stroking me. I hated myself so fucking much."

"Why?" I ask when he doesn't continue for a minute. I know what he is about to say but I know he needs to be the one to say it.

"Because I got hard." He spits the words out like they burn his tongue. "I fucking came in his hand and there wasn't a fucking thing that I could do about it!" He yanks his hand from mine and stands. He paces the room muttering beneath his breath, so low I can't make out the words. Bob stirs beside me and I quickly pat him so he'll fall back asleep or else he will pee in my room if I don't take him right away to the bathroom. "I got hard when he sucked me off as well and like the bitch that I am, I fucking came down his throat hating myself even fucking more for being so weak."

"You're not weak! Anyone in your position would have done the same thing, you were a prisoner–"

"No!" He shouts, his raised voice wakes Bob and I quickly pluck him up and cradle him against my chest. "You don't get it. I don't fucking like dudes nor have I ever wanted to–to touch one, and some Russian cunt comes along making me hard and forcing me to come! What the fuck does that make me? Am I gay? Did I fucking like him playing with my cock?" I can't stand the distance between us so I climb off the bed and as much as I hate what I'm about to do, I know Rook needs me more in this moment, so I put Bob in the bathroom and close the door. At least cleaning his pee will be easier if he does it on the tiles instead of the carpet in my room. I eliminate the space between Rook and I, then reach out, hoping he can see what I'm about to do and grab his hands in mine. I hate that he won't let me turn the light on so I can see him.

"Listen to me. You are not gay. You are not weak and you sure as hell didn't ask for anything that happened to you. I am so fucking sorry that you went through that ordeal. I wish more than anything it never happened, but we can't sit here and think about the shoulda-coulda-woul- das. We have to face it and I want you to know that I will be here every step of the way."

"How can you stand to be near me after what I just told you? I sucked his cock, Clare. He fucked me raw and made me come more times than I can count. If I fought back, I wound up being chained to a wall and beaten until I passed out. He would cut me and make me bleed just so he could use my blood as lube. I was starved and left to rot. The only way to get food or water from that cunt was to beg him to fuck me!" Tears trek down my cheeks. I bite my lip to stop the sob from tearing out of me at hearing what he had to endure. "I fucking begged for his cock in my ass!" His voice hitches, then when I hear him sniffle, I'm done for. I spin around and hit the light switch. Rook crumples into a heap on the floor as sobs tear out of him. I launch myself at him and wrap my arms around his shaking form fighting back tears of my own. "You need to leave, Clare."

My arms stiffen around him. "I'm not leaving you," I say in a tone that leaves no room for argument. His arms wrap around me in a vice-like grip.

"I'm no good for you anymore." He hiccups and I tighten my hold on him, then rest my chin atop his head as he nuzzles his face into the crook of my neck.

"That isn't your call to make." I take a shuddering breath and push past the lump in my throat. "You can push me away but I won't leave you."

"I've been so angry at you and blamed you because I thought you ran from me and killed our baby." I slam my eyes closed and breathe through the pain that this topic brings with it. I may have been young but I wanted that baby more than he will ever know. "I wanted to hurt you because I blamed you. I thought if you had just stayed and not ran, my life would have taken a different path and I would never have been angry and bitter enough to do what I did with Koby. I replay that night over and over in my mind. I should never have gone to the docks and none of this would have happened."

"Imagine if you didn't go to the docks though. Your brother would never have gone to Russia and saved the lives of all those girls. I know what you went through was traumatic but you going through what you did saved the lives of thousands of innocent women and children."

Chapter Fifteen

I pull back from her embrace and mull over her words. I have never thought about it the way she has said it. Would those girls and Anya still be stuck in Russia at the mercy of Vlad and Ivan if I wasn't taken? Yeah, they would be. I use the backs of my hands to brush away the tears and fight the embarrassment that thrums through me at crying in front of Clare. I tentatively reach out and cup her tear-stained cheeks between my hands. I search her gaze, trying to get a read on what she is thinking but all I see is... love. She doesn't look at me with disgust or shudder at my touch like I thought she would after hearing all of that.

"I want to kiss you." My eyes widen in surprise at the same time hers do, she is just as taken back by my statement as I am.

"You never have to ask to kiss me." Her voice has turned raspy and I hear the undercurrent of lust in her tone.

"I haven't... I mean, I..." She presses her index finger against my lips and smiles shyly.

"If it makes you feel any better, I've never been with anyone else except... you." My brows jump up to my hairline. Clare and I were each other's firsts so that means...

"You never slept with anyone else after you... left?" She nods and that one action has heat spreading throughout my body. I don't think I just act. I smash my lips against hers—she gasps in shock. I use that to my advantage and plunge my tongue inside her mouth. The moment my tongue brushes hers, a moan slips free. She reaches out and grips the front of my shirt pulling me closer. I skate my hands all over her, loving how her skin feels beneath my touch and when it pebbles with goose flesh, I smirk against her mouth.

I grip her hips and gently lift her so she straddles my waist. She rests her hands on the tops of my shoulders as she grinds down against my erection. My breath hitches and I pull back, breaking the kiss as I take a deep breath and remind myself Clare isn't Ivan. She cups my cheeks and lifts my face to hers. I slam my eyes closed not wanting to see a pitying look in her eyes.

"Look at me," she urges. I take a minute to gather myself before slowly blinking my eyes open and peering up at her. There is no trace of pity in her eyes just... understanding. "Whatever you need from me, just say. If you want to stop and go watch movies, we can do that but just know, there is no pressure from me." Her words start to ease the tension coiling inside me. My grip on her hips tighten as I make the final decision to not allow Ivan to take this moment from me. I have allowed that fucker too much of my head space. I loved sex and being balls deep inside pussy, but ever since being in Russia, I cower at the thought of sex or even getting hard. I haven't even jacked myself off in months because I was too scared that it would trigger a flashback! I blow out a loud exhale and decide this is the moment where I take control of my life back and not allow my past to ruin any chance of me having a future.

"I need you to not stop unless I say otherwise, don't treat me differently." She nods and smiles proudly down at me as she cups my cheeks.

"Let me be your anchor, allow me to keep you grounded and I promise you, everything will be okay." I claim her lips and watch as her eyes flutter closed. I don't follow her lead, keeping mine open and watching her. I need to see her so she can ground me like only she can. Clare has always been a part of me. I tried to mask the pain of her leaving by hiding behind humor and fucking my way through the female population, but the truth is, they meant nothing to me. They were just an escape to ease the ache in my heart that losing her caused. I just had no idea that Tony was the fucking cause of me losing my first and only love.

She runs her fingers through my hair and I moan at the feeling of her exploring my body. I skate my hands down her body until I'm cupping her ass and climb to my feet. She locks her legs around my hips and doesn't break our kiss as I move us to the bed. I gently lay her down and smile when I see the annoyed look on her face from me putting distance between us.

"Just let me take in the sight of you, ready and waiting for me." Her eyes soften at my words. I've never cared about looking at or even wanting to remember any of the others but Clare isn't just anyone, she is *my* person. She reaches down and pops the button on her shorts. I stand here and watch her, transfixed on the sight in front of me. Clare has no idea what a fucking goddess she truly is. She shimmies her sleep shorts down her legs and my mouth waters at the sight of her bare pussy. "No panties?" She bites her bottom lip and shakes her head.

"I never wear them to bed." I groan and fight the urge to palm my cock through my jeans. I can see her thighs are slick with her arousal. I'm a slave to my own body, I bend down and lick her inner thighs cleaning them. The moment the taste of her explodes on my tongue, a long throaty moan tears from deep within me.

"Fuck, you taste so good, baby." A small moan comes from her. I smirk as I continue to lick her thighs purposely avoiding the place she wants my tongue the most. I reach up and push her shirt up, exposing her stomach, I glide over her pussy and love when she growls in protest. I place a tender kiss to the scar on her abdomen and force the anger I feel away, knowing that this isn't the time to let my rage toward Tony out. I wish it was me that killed the fucker! She lifts up helping me rid her of her shirt. I bite my lip and I wedge myself between her legs. I release my lip and smirk when I pull the cups of her bra down. My eyes widen and my gaze shoots to hers. "Since when do you have your nipples pierced?"

A blush coats her cheeks as she shrugs. "I got them done last year." I cup her tits in my hands and flick my thumbs over her nipples, loving the fact that they are pierced.

"I fucking love them but you'll never allow anyone else to see what is *mine* again!" Her eyes glaze over with raw need.

"*Yours,* huh?" she sass's. I pinch her nipples between my fingers and relish in the breathy moan that escapes her as her back arches off the bed.

"Make no mistake, baby, you've always been mine, even

when you didn't know it. You and I are cosmic, we're destiny." I don't wait for a response as I bend down and flick my tongue over her nipple. The sound that comes from her has my cock rock hard and straining against my jeans, begging for me to bury it inside her tight wet hole. I suck her nipple into my mouth and swirl my tongue around her peak at the same time.

"Shit!" she cries out as she bucks her hips off the bed trying to grind against me. I grip her waist with my free hand and pin her to the bed as I continue to lap at her nipple. I release it with a wet pop and switch to the other side, clamping my teeth down on her metal bar and relishing in the gasp that escapes her. She grips my hair and tugs on the strands, pulling me in closer. I take her hint and bite down harder on her nipple. "Oh my God!" she cries out. I release her nipple and slide up her body until I capture her lips in a kiss that brands her as mine. She reaches down and grips the hem of my shirt and pulls it up. I try not to tense when I help her pull it the remainder of the way off. I rest back on my haunches and fight the urge to hide my marred body from her. She reaches up and runs the tips of her fingers all over me tracing the lines that will remain on my skin forever.

"I can keep the shirt on," I offer. She glares up at me, her nose twitches which tells me she is pissed.

"I told you before, you're beautiful and I want all of you." She doesn't give me a chance to protest when she grips the waistband of my jeans and pops the button while never taking her eyes off mine. The sound of my zipper being pulled down is the only sound that can be heard. My breath stills when she pushes them down. I help her out and slip off the bed as I push my jeans down and stand before her in my black briefs. I stare down at her and whatever she sees in my gaze has her shuffling her naked ass off the bed and dropping to her knees before me.

"I'm going to help you out of these," she says as she grips the waistband of my briefs but doesn't move to pull them down. "I'm going to keep my hands at my sides and you are going to be in full control." I open my mouth to speak but she shakes her head causing me to clamp it closed as she continues. "This is about *you*, not me. Next time though, it will definitely be all about me, I can promise you that."

She will never know how much I appreciate her words and how she can sense my unease without me ever having to say anything. She slowly eases my briefs down my legs, my cock springs free and slaps angrily against my stomach. It's been a minute since I have looked at my cock and felt anything but disgust but the way Clare looks at it—like she is starving for a taste—has a whole different sensation of feelings thrumming through me. I step out of my boxers and watch as she licks her lips and swallows a few times as if her mouth is watering. Gripping the base of my cock, I hiss at the contact. I pump myself and groan, picturing what it's going to feel like having Clare's lips wrapped around me after so many years.

"Open your mouth and keep your arms locked behind your back." She does as I ask without delay. I slip my dick inside her mouth and bite down on my lip to keep from groaning. She begins to shake her head but Clare forgets I know she doesn't have a gag reflex and takes me all the way into the back of her throat. Once I am fully sheathed inside her mouth I finally let my moan of pleasure slip free. She peeks up at me through her lashes, asking without words if she can move. "Suck me deep, baby." She hollows her cheeks and clamps her lips tight around my cock as she bobs up and down on it like a fucking pro! I want to close my eyes and bask in the feelings but I'm too frightened I'll trigger myself. As if she can sense my wayward thoughts she defies me and reaches out to grip the sides of my legs pulling me back into the present. I lock gazes with her and immediately all thoughts except how she is making me feel remain.

"Hmmm," she moans around my cock, the vibrations sending shock waves up my spine and causing me to shiver.

"Fuck yeah, baby. Take me all the way!" I breathe out. She does as I ask and fuck me, I nearly come on the spot. I yank my cock free of her mouth. She pouts up at me. The sight of her spit dripping down her chin and the tears in her eyes from taking me so deep have me smiling. "You've never looked so beautiful as you do now." In answer she lifts her index finger and swipes the spit from her chin then sucks it clean. I growl my approval. "Get on the bed and open your legs wide." Her eyes haze over with need as she rushes to do as I say. She climbs on the bed, balancing her ass on the edge, then bends her legs at the knee and opens them as wide as she can, giving me the picture-perfect view of her pink pussy.

Chapter Sixteen

My body is brimming with need, the taste of his pre-cum still coats my tongue. I have to force myself not to moan at the taste of him. His cock is hard and ready, resting against his stomach. A shiver rolls through me at the thought of having him inside me again after so long. He rests his hands on the tops of my knees as he stares down at my pussy. I know I'm dripping wet and I can't find it within myself to give a fuck that he can see how much I want him. Rook is the only man to have ever been inside me and I plan to make him the last. He says I am his but the truth of the matter is he has always been mine as well. There is no one else in this world that could put me through hell and still get me naked in the same night.

He shifts and runs a single finger through my slicks

folds causing me to cry out and buck my hips off the bed. I watch in a hazy state of arousal as he brings that single digit to his mouth and sucks it clean, moaning the whole time. I try to clench my thighs together, to alleviate the ache that is now becoming painful, but he snaps his hands out, grips my knees and holds my legs wide open while pinning me with a disapproving glare.

"You don't move until I tell you to." I groan in annoyance. Rook strikes out so fucking fast I don't even have to comprehend what just happened until I cry out from him smacking my pussy. "Don't you dare rush me! I'm going to take my time devouring this fucking pussy and you are going to take everything I give you, got it?" I wish I could say I fought him and took control but I can't. My pussy gushes with my wetness and my nipples turn to stone just from the commanding tone of his voice. "Answer me."

"Yes, I got it." He smiles triumphantly down at me.

"Good girl, now get ready to scream while I eat this cunt until you come and then I'm going to fill you with my cock until you are writhing and squirting all over my dick, baby." I can't help the blush that coats my cheeks. Rook and I figured out I was a squirter the third time we had sex and it became his favorite game to see how many times he could get me to squirt each time we were together. Watching this beautiful, tortured man drop to his knees in front of me steals my breath. He grips my legs and pushes them wider, my pussy right in line with his face. When he darts his tongue out to swipe through my slick folds, I'm powerless to stop the moan from tearing from me. "Fuck!" he moans before burying his face between my legs and eating me like the most delectable meal he has ever had.

"Oh my God," I cry out as I grind against his face, rocking my hips in motion with his tongue. My body begins to heat all over as he brings me closer to the edge of my climax. I can feel my pending orgasm and try to latch onto it but I need... more. As if he can sense my melancholy, he inserts a single finger inside me causing me to gasp and almost choke on my own breath.

"Fuck, you're so tight." All I can do is moan in answer, too caught up in the feelings he is inflicting on my body. He sucks my clit into his mouth as he pumps his finger inside me at a punishing rate. He tears my orgasm from me. I scream his name so fucking loud, I swear Knight and Koby will be able to hear me from next door. I feel the pressure in my pussy building as he continues to suck my clit and finger fuck me. He yanks his finger free and I squirt all over his naked chest. "Fuck yes," he growls. The minute I stop gushing, I slouch back into the bed panting. Rook stands and I watch as he licks his lips and moans his approval. "I fucking missed that." That is all he says before climbing on top of me.

I widen my legs to accommodate him. He bends down and kisses me. I wrap my arms around his neck as I swipe my tongue against his, tasting my own release. I've always loved the taste of my own orgasm. I suck his tongue and moan at the taste of my come on his tongue. He doesn't break our kiss as he reaches between us and lines his cock up with my opening. I try not to tense but it has been years since I've had sex. I won't lie, either I'm not remembering clearly or the size of Rook's cock has grown in four years. When I feel the head of his cock at my entrance, my grip around his neck tightens as I brace myself for him to slam inside me.

When his pushes inside me I gasp into his mouth. He breaks our kiss and rests his forehead against mine. We gaze into the other's eyes and I can tell from the look in his brown eyes that he is fighting to stay present with me and not allow what happened to him ruin this moment. So I decide to not think and just say what's on my mind.

"I love you." The air rushes out of him. "I want this with you." His eyes close. "I'll always want you. Even when you push me away, I'll always come back to you because you. Rook Murdoch, are the end to *my* story." His eyes snap open, he takes a deep breath, his eyes spark with life then he slams inside me, causing us both to cry out. He buries his face in the crook of my neck as we both breath through the feeling of being joined together as one again. He gives me a minute to adjust to him before he rests up on his arms, putting them on either side of my head. I see the sheen of sweat that covers his forehead and know this is hard for him to remain still and not move.

He darts his eyes to mine. When a look of indecision crosses his face, I smile up at him and decide to throw him a bone. "Don't say anything right now, just feel and share this moment with me." He nods then begins to move inside me. I lock my legs around his waist as I reach up and scarp my nails along his back.

"Fuck, keep doing that," he rasps out. I do as he says and continue to drag my nails along his back as he shudders from touch. "I need to fuck you, baby. I'm not gonna last so I can't go slow right now." His tone is clipped and I know without a doubt he is already on the verge of coming.

"Fuck me hard and come, babe, then you can make it up to me later." And he does, he fucks me so hard and deep that I swear there will be an imprint of my body on the mattress for the next week. I can feel another orgasm building. He grips my hair and pulls it hard until my neck is bare to him. He bites down on the tender flesh between my shoulder and neck and sucks hard, branding me as his. I feel his cock swelling inside me and try with all my might to grasp my orgasm but I'm too late, he comes roaring my name. I keep the disappointed look from my face as he pulls out of me and slips off the bed. I attempt to close my legs but he pushes them open and shoves two fingers inside me pulling a cry from me.

"I want you to come all over my fucking fingers, baby, then you'll come on my cock next time." As if I am a puppet having its master pull her strings, I come on command screaming his name until my throat is hoarse. He yanks his fingers free and immediately jumps back as I drench the bed in my own cum. His eyes are ablaze with lust as he stares down at me in amazement, so I do the only thing I can think of to toy with him. I reach down between my legs and swipe a single finger through my folds coating it with my own release then bring it to my mouth and suck it clean while he watches me the whole time with a heated look in his eyes. "Get on your knees and suck my cock. I need to fuck you again so you can suck your cum off my cock."

I WAKE to the feeling of his wet mouth wrapped around my nipple and smile. I blink my eyes open when I hear him chuckle and roll on top of me. He pushes my legs apart with his knees as he makes himself at home. Looking up at him this morning, I don't see any of the darkness in his eyes, it seems like a weight has been lifted off of him and that has my heart soaring.

"Morning, sunshine." I furrow my brow.

"Sunshine?" I question. He ducks his head and peers up at me through his long black lashes that make me jealous— he has natural perfect lashes and I don't.

"Seems like a fitting name for you."

"Why?" I push. He blows out a long exhale, clearly uncomfortable with admitting why he has chosen that nickname. I reach up and grip his chin, bringing his gaze back to me. "Tell me."

"Because you are the *sunshine* to my darkness, the light to my dark if you will so, I thought it was the perfect name for you." I don't know why, but his words have tears springing to my eyes. "I've yearned for you for years, Clare. I need you to know that I am so sorry for how I've treated you—" I try to cut in but he shakes his head. I close my mouth and listen. "I'm going to make it up to you. I love you, Clare, and I want a future with you." Tears leak from the corners of my eyes. "I want the future that was robbed from us years ago, starting with you being able to achieve your dreams." My brow dips in confusion. "I had some help, but I enrolled you in school and paid off your father's medical bills." I open my mouth ready to scream and shout at him for going behind my back, my father's medical bills were over eight-hundred thousand dollars. He slams his lips against mine. I keep my mouth clamped shut but when he pushes his cock inside me, I gasp, granting him the entry he wanted. The moment he begins to move inside me, all thought flees my mind as he evokes this fucking incredible euphoric bliss with my body. Within mere minutes he has me coming all over his cock and screaming his name so loud I swear I wake the whole fucking Murdoch family.

Chapter Seventeen

Clare took the rest of the week off work and we have spent the past three days holed up in my house, fucking on every possible surface. I made sure she knew clothes were optional. She protested and said there were too many windows and my family might see, I of course showed her the amazing button that turns the glass black so we can see out but no one can see in. It's Friday and I plan to spend the whole weekend like I have spent the past three days–inside her. Spending this time with Clare has helped me more than she will ever know. I've blown Opal off and not bothered to even accept her calls or texts. Clare turned her phone off and laughed saying that no one calls her anyway.

I'm sitting on the couch with nothing but a throw blanket over me and Clare tucked into my side wearing one of my shirts, Bob cuddled up against her legs. I fucking love seeing her in my clothes. She's ignoring me at the moment as she tries to act engrossed in the movie, pissed off because I keep ripping every pair of panties off her when she puts them on. Apparently, the yellow pair I ripped off her forty minutes ago was her last pair. I shrugged, not giving a fuck, then proceeded to fuck her on the counter. Apparently, me fucking her brains out didn't cause her to forget she no longer owns any pairs of panties.

"So—"

"No!" She cuts me off, I glare down at the top of her head.

"You don't even know what I was going to say!" I protest.

"Yeah, I do." I narrow my eyes at her.

"Oh, what was I going to say then, smartass?" She shifts and stares up at me with a look that has me forcing a smile and cupping my dick. Clare has a fucking temper and the girl isn't above dick punching me, she's done it before!

"Let me *fuck you better*." She mimics how I sound and I scoff.

"I don't sound like that!" She quirks a brow mockingly.

"No, you just sound like a whining baby who lost their favorite toy." I mock gasp and place a hand over my heart.

"Are you threatening to take *my* pussy from me?" She throws her arms up in the air and jumps up from the couch, ready to storm out of the room. I'm quicker than her. I wrap my arm around her waist and haul her back down, laying her on the couch beneath me. Bob yelps and leaps off the couch. I fight the smile that wants to break free knowing I just pissed the rat off. Clare tries to shove me off, so I grab both her wrists in one hand and pin them above her head as I nestle myself between her delicious thighs. She can try to act pissed off all she wants but with no panties on and me being butt naked, I can feel how wet she is against my cock.

"Don't you dare put that *thing* inside me," she warns.

"Now, that is a low blow calling RJ a *thing*." Her face scrunches in disgust.

"Did you just name your cock, *RJ*, as in Rook Junior?" I smile wide and puff my chest up as I answer.

"Sure did, sunshine." Her mouth unhinges. I grind against her bare pussy and fight the smirk that wants to break free when she bites down on her bottom lip to keep from moaning.

"Could RJ put some fucking clothes on!" At the sound of my brother's voice, I still on top of Clare and blindly reach behind me for the throw blanket and pull it over us. I shoot her an apologetic look as she buries her face in my chest and I turn to see all four of my brothers standing the entry way with different looks of disgust on their faces. "I could have gone my lifetime without knowing you named your dick that," Knight says as he fake shudders.

"What the hell are you all doing here?" I snap, pissed off that they just walked into *my* house unannounced. I don't give a fuck if they see my brown ass but I do give a fuck that they see Clare in just my shirt. Gage and King both turn to look at Bishop who pins me with an annoyed stare.

"Opal called, said you haven't been answering her calls —" I cut in not wanting to get a fucking lecture from my brother.

"As you can see, I've been a bit preoccupied. Now, if that's all, can you lot fuck off?" I bite out.

"Not nice when someone walks in on you and your girl, is it?" Knight interjects, I pin my twin with a look that I hope conveys he is pushing too fucking far right now.

"Please, it got you harder knowing I was watching you fuck Koby." Bishop, King and Gage groan but don't comment. Knight's eyes blaze with rage—good, get angry brother because I am ready to fucking go.

"The crows want Ivan back!" Gage cuts in before Knight and I can get into it further. At the mention of Ivan my blood runs cold and I turn to stone above Clare. My breaths turned ragged and my mind reels with images of my time with him. Before I can recede too far into the past and get lost in my own mind, the feeling of her tiny hands cupping my face and pulling my gaze back to hers pulls me out of my spiral.

"Come back to me." Her whispered words wash over me and remind me that I'm *here*, I'm not back in Russia being... Ivan's *pet*. "Don't let him pull you back into the darkness. Stay with me and let me be your *sunshine*." Taking a deep breath I nod and keep my gaze on her as I speak to my brothers.

"Wait outside. I need to dress and then we'll talk."

SITTING HERE in Bishop's office I start to feel claustrophobic. I dig my nails into the palm of my hand to keep me focused. Bishop refused to allow Clare in on the meeting which set me off but Clare being the saint she is, said she would hang with the girls and wait for me. So, I now sit here in the office with Gage, Bish, Knight and King. When the door opens, I peer over my shoulder shocked as shit to see my sister storming into the office like she is about to tear shit up. Car has a furious look on her face and is staring directly at Bish. We may be the muscle and brawn in this family but the truth is, Carlina Murelo is the one that has the true Italian temper and is trigger happy.

"Gucci!" Vin rushes in after his wife with his daughter clutched to his chest and an annoyed look in his eyes. Car ignores him as she pushes between mine and Knight's seats to place both her hands on Bishop's desk. She folds slightly so they are eye level. Vincent groans behind his wife but is smart enough to remain quiet or risk her turning her ire on him.

"What can I do for you, sister?" Bishop asks as he reclines back in his chair with his hands clasped in front of him.

"*What can I do for you, sister?*" Car mocks, trying to sound like Bishop. Gage and King snicker in the corner. "Well for one, when you decide to host a family *pow-wow* with my baby brother, don't you think I should know about it?" Bishop's left eye twitches as he tries to remain calm and not bite our sister's head off. Unlike Tony, none of us ever lay hands on our women or sister—unless it's in the bedroom, then we all get fucking handsy.

"Carlina, you are a mother and have a child—"

Car cuts Bish off. "She has a father who is quite fucking capable of looking after her. You forget who I am married to, brother. They don't call him the bloodhound for nothing and I assure you, Vincent never misses the kill shot—well, unless it's me, then my baby can't aim for shit." Vincent growls at how smug his wife sounds when she says that.

"I missed on purpose," he grumbles behind her. She turns and smirks up at her baby daddy and winks.

"I know, baby. You keep telling yourself whatever you need to sleep at night." Vin turns an angry shade of red but it doesn't reach his eyes. He can talk a big game but we all know Vincent would never hurt Carlina, he can't. He is too far gone when it comes to her. Vincent is the type of guy to burn cities down if anyone ever tried to come for his wife or daughter.

Bishop cuts in before they can go at it more. "Fine." Car turns back to B with a devious smirk on her lips.

"Now, was that so hard?" Bish growls and pins her with a scathing look. She smartly clamps her mouth closed, knowing not to push Bishop too far or he will snap. "Baby, take Channel out in the living room with the others, I won't be long." Most men would bristle and argue about their wives telling them what to do in a room full of men but not Vin. He places a chaste kiss to her lips and warns her to be good before leaving the room with his baby. Car plants her ass on the armrest of my chair and waves her arm for Bishop to continue, which just earns her a snarl from the big bastard.

"The crows want Ivan back." At the mention of Ivan, Car rests her hand on my shoulder offering me her silent support. I reach up and rest my hand atop hers. A small gasp escapes her at the contact but no one comments.

"Why?" Knight asks with a trace of anger lacing his words.

Bishop meets my gaze as he answers. "They say the Russian's are getting antsy waiting for his death."

I narrow my eyes at my brother, reading between the lines. "You gave them a timeline on his death and the deadline is approaching, isn't it?" He exhales loudly and nods. I shake my head in disgust. "Who the fuck are you to give *me* a timeframe, Bishop?"

"He didn't have a choice, Rook." King tries to defend our brother. I turn and shoot him a scathing look.

"Did you give Ally a timeline with Pauly and Donny, or am I just the lucky one?" King's eyes blaze with contempt.

He tries to take a step toward me but Gage stops him with a hand on his chest. I scoff and turn back to the Don. "How long?"

"You have a week to get it done or—" I cut Bishop off, knowing exactly what he is going to say next.

"You'll do it so our family doesn't look weak." Bishop nods. There is no way he can send Ivan back to Russia alive. Me not being able to kill him means my weakness will be projected onto our family and that is something as the head of the family Bishop can't allow.

"I'm sorry, Rook." I turn to Gage perplexed why he is sorry. "Anya fought for you to be able to do this at your own pace but she is no longer the head of the Bratva and Andreas overruled her." Hearing this gives me pause. I don't even really know Anya Volkov. I mean, we share a fucked-up connection because of what we went through together when Ivan held her captive, but I never expected her to go to bat for me.

"I'll do it." I snap my gaze to my other side and pin Knight with a glare, but he's focused on Bishop. "You need to have a live feed, right?" Bishop nods causing me to grit my teeth. Those fuckers want to watch me exact my revenge on the bastard that tortured me! "I'll do it. They'll never be able to tell the difference between me and Rook." I brush Car's hand off me as I stand and meet Bish's concerned stare.

"I'll be ready in three days. I'll send you a list of what I'll need." I turn, ready to flee the confines of this space when Bishop speaks, halting my movements.

"When this is over, we are going to sit down and work out this hate you have toward me, King and Knight. I can't have us divided—" I keep my back to him as I cut the fucker off.

"Yeah, I know why you need this sorted, Bishop. You want to take Miami from Anthony and you want me as the head of the Murelo territory so Car can step down." I peer over my shoulder to find him looking at me with wide eyes. "I know everything. You may think I've had my head buried in the sand for months but I haven't. I know everything you have in motion. You want the rest of us to step up so you can control Miami and New York making us the most powerful family in the continental US."

Clare

I shouldn't be standing outside Bishop's office eavesdropping but when I heard Knight speak about killing Ivan on a live video feed for Rook, I couldn't help it.

"Yeah, I know why you need this sorted Bishop. You want to take Miami from Anthony and you want me as the head of the Murelo territory so Car can step down." The anguish in his voice spears me right in the heart, he can't do this. "I know everything, you may think I've had my head buried in the sand for months but I haven't. I know everything you have in motion. You want the rest of us to step up so you can control Miami and New York making us the most powerful family in the continental US." At the sound of his retreating footsteps, I quickly race into the kitchen and pour myself a glass of water to act like I wasn't just spying. Rook comes into the kitchen a second later, the look in his dark gaze tells me I'm so busted. "You heard all of that?"

I don't bother lying, I nod. "Yeah," I say as he scrubs a hand down his face and nods.

"Come on, I have to do something." I don't question him, he reaches his hand out to me and I take it without hesitation knowing I would follow this man into the depths of hell without blinking. He leads us out of the kitchen, passing his brothers and sister as we head for the front door. At the sound of laughter coming from the living room, he pauses then changes directions and heads toward the sound of laughter with his siblings following after us.

When we enter the living room everyone is where I left them. Koby, Anya and Ally are all sitting on the floor with the twins who are playing on their playmat. Kiara and Vin sit on the three-seater sofa with Amelia between them as she keeps darting her gaze between them both staring at her cousins, that Vin and Kiara each have clutched to their chests as they sleep. At the sight, a pang hits me square in the chest. What would our baby have looked like? All conversation stops and all eyes turn to us. Knight and the others step around us and go to join their partners and kids, making them all look like the picture-perfect family.

"Anya." Her gaze flickers from Gage to Rook, looking confused as hell as she stares up at Rook. Gage slips in behind her, wraps his arms around her waist and pulls her flush against his chest as she rests between his legs. "Thank you." Her brow furrows slightly confused by Rook's grate-fulness. "I-I didn't help... you." He blows out an exasperated breath. I squeeze his hand letting him know I'm right here with him. "But you still tried to help me and... I'm sorry I didn't—" Anya pulls free of Gage's hold as she stands and moves toward Rook. Knowing that this is *their* moment, I pull free of his hold and step back so she and him can have some semblance of privacy. She reaches out and tentatively grips his hands in hers, I can tell her touch makes him uneasy but he doesn't pull back and that makes me so proud of him.

"You have absolutely *nothing* to be sorry for." The conviction in her tone is awe inspiring.

He shakes his head denying her claim. "You stopped what was happening to me and turned *his* attention back to you, why?" The anger in his voice is felt by everyone but it isn't directed at Anya.

"I mean this with all due respect. I knew I could handle it. I saw the look in your eyes, Rook, and knew you were at the breaking point and I couldn't allow that to happen."

"Why?" he whispers. Everyone in the room is waiting with bated breath for her reply, she smiles at him.

"I may not have known you then, I still don't really and that's okay, but I felt like I got to know you through Gage. My love for him meant I had to do something to help his little brother, even if it was the last thing I did." I turn to Gage to see he is just as surprised as Rook hearing this revelation. Rook pulls his hands back and shocks everyone when he pulls Anya to him and... hugs her. They both are stiff for a few seconds before they relax into the embrace. Tears cloud my vision at the sight before me—he is healing and he doesn't even know it yet.

"Thank you for saving me. You had no idea but I had managed to get hold of a blade from that trolley and planned to end my suffering that night." Gasps sound out around the room. Anya pulls back and cups his face between her hands. A shuddering breath escapes him as he closes his eyes, clearly embarrassed by his declaration. He keeps his eyes closed as he continues on. "What you did for me, stopped me from giving into my demons."

"Look at me!" Her voice leaves no room for argument, Rook slowly blinks his eyes open and stares at her. "I didn't save you, *you* saved yourself! What you went through, none of us will ever understand. We can empathize with you but we can never relate because everyone experiences things differently." A lump forms in my throat when I see his eyes fill with moisture. "You are stronger than you even know. What Andreas is asking of you is my fault. I had the chance to end his life but I didn't because you need to do this." I cringe at her telling him he needs to murder his molester. "He can't hurt you anymore, Rook. If you want... I'll be there with you the whole time."

"I'd... I would be... yes." Is all he says before she pulls him to her again. Dread begins to pool inside me. He can't seriously be considering taking someone's life, can he?

AFTER WE LEFT THE OTHERS, Rook drove us into the city and refused to tell me where we were going. I was shocked to my core when he parked in front of a tattoo studio and told me it was time to bury his scars. I didn't know what the hell he meant until he explained, he's covering the scars Ivan left on him with ink. He says this is his way of moving on from his past. Seeing his scars every day is a constant reminder of what he went through so he wants them covered so he never has to see them again. We've been here for hours. Every time I hear the tattoo guns buzz, I flinch. I don't know how he can stand to have two men working on him at the same time.

I marvel at the sight of his body, now covered in ink—his

arms, chest and neck is tattooed. They are now halfway through doing his back and I'll admit, God, the ink looks good on him. When I came here months ago to see Luka about dad, Rook looked skinny and malnourished but since he's been working out at Gage's gym—the one he now runs —he's begun to fill out again and pile back on his muscles. His six-pack is even beginning to take shape again. Rook's beauty is raw, one look at him and he steals the very breath from my lungs which is why, I have to convince him that killing Ivan isn't the answer. I may love him but I cannot condone murder. I know who his family is but he has always been different than them.

"SUNSHINE?" I moan and try to brush away the feeling of him shaking me awake. "Baby, wake up." I groan and open my eyes, then sit up in fright when I realize I fell asleep on the couch at the tattoo parlor. I run my gaze over Rook to see he has his shirt back on and a sexy as all hell smirk on his lips.

"Sorry, I must have been more tired than I thought," I say before a yawn slips free. He smiles and helps me up. He thanks the guys as we head out. Before we leave the shop, he stops and slips his sweater over my head. The smell of him immediately surrounds me and I sigh in contentment. He interlaces our fingers as we make our way back to the car. I can't help but smile. I never thought Rook and I would ever find our way back to one another. I mean, I had hoped we would but I just never thought it would be possible after what happened. When we reach his Land Rover Defender, he pops the locks and opens the door for me to slip inside. I swoon when he reaches across me and buckles me in. He pulls back and the heated look in his eyes sends a shiver down my spine. I'm powerless to stop myself. I lean forward and kiss him, long and slow, making sure he can tell just from this kiss that I *need* him inside me.

He breaks our kiss on a groan. I'm breathless and hot all over. I squirm in my seat as I try to alleviate the ache between my thighs. "Fuck, this is gonna be a long drive," he grumbles as he closes the door and heads to his side, then starts the car and pulls out. Two minutes into the drive and I'm hyper aware of how close he is to me. I need to touch him. I reach over and run my hand over the top of his dick and gasp when I feel how hard he is already. "Just looking at you gets me rock fucking hard." I smile triumphantly, it's still so hard to comprehend someone like me can get this God of a man off. "Either move your fucking hand or pull it out and make me come!" His heated words has a thrill shooting through me. I unbuckle my seat belt and lean over the console to undo his jeans. I can feel his gaze boring a hole into the top of my head, he doesn't stop me though.

I peel his zipper down and pull his cock free. He hisses at the feeling of me touching him. His cock is angry and red, my mouth watering at the sight of him. I don't draw this out, knowing we both need it. He needs to release his pent up stress and I need to taste him more than I need my next breath. I wrap my lips around his head, sucking him all the way into the back of my throat. I love the sounds he makes, the taste of him and hearing his dirty words has me clamping my thighs together. I can feel how wet I am already. I have no panties on and know I must have a wet spot on the front of my light-blue jeans.

"Fuck yes, baby, like that," he rasps out as he grips the back of my head and pushes me all the way down on his cock. He's always loved that I don't have a gag reflex and can take him all the way inside my mouth. "Fuck!" he shouts. I gasp around his cock when I feel the car swerve. I try to pull back but his grip on my head won't allow it. He reaches around me and slams the car in park before pushing his chair back and then thrusting into my mouth. My worries of us crashing flee knowing that he must have pulled over somewhere. "Fuck yes, you suck like a fucking porn star, baby." I moan around his cock. "You want my cum inside your pussy or down your throat." He releases his hold on my head allowing me to pull back. I look around to find we're parked in a dark alley.

There is just enough light in the car for me to see his heated gaze is on me. I make quick work of freeing myself of my pants, as Rook pushes his further down his legs before I hop across the console and straddle him. His hands immediately go to my hips. I push up as much as I can, given the space in the car, and line his cock up with my entrance. I slowly lower onto him, gasping. Rook hisses at the feeling of his cock slipping inside my tight wet hole.

"Fuck!" I moan out when he is fully sheathed inside me, just the feeling of having him buried deep inside my pussy has me wanting to come.

"You're so fucking tight, sunshine," he growls out. He pushes my shirt up and smirks when he sees I'm not wearing a bra. He doesn't waste time. He leans forward and sucks my nipple into his mouth, causing me to cry out. My body moves of its own accord and my hips begin to rock back and forward making us both moan. He releases my nipple with a wet pop then claims my lips in a searing kiss. I reach up to grip the handle above the door for something to hold onto as I ride him. He drops back into his seat, tweaks my nipples between his fingers and that sets me off. I stop moving, fighting off my orgasm not wanting to ruin the interior of his car. I can feel his disapproving gaze on me but ignore it. I start to move again but at a slower pace. After a minute, I start to bounce up and down again on his cock, moaning shamelessly at the feeling he is inflicting on my body. When I feel my orgasm cresting again I stop moving. He growls out in anger. "What the fuck are you doing?" he snaps.

"I... I–."

"I swear to God if you don't squirt all over my dick in the next minute you won't be coming for a month!" I gape down at him shocked he would threaten me with that.

"It will go everywhere and ruin your car!" I protest, he grips my hips in a punishing hold and begins to slam inside me, I cry out.

"I don't give a fuck." He rasps out, in my frenzied state of bliss I forget about his fresh ink and claw at his chest. He hisses but doesn't protest. If anything his thrusts grow more erratic. I feel my orgasm building again and this time he won't allow me to stop. He slams inside me two more times before I scream out, lifting me off his cock as I squirt all over him. He hums his approval, but doesn't give me a chance to calm down as he slams back inside.

"Rook!" I scream out.

"Take it baby, take every fucking thing I give you, sunshine," he grits out as he continues to fuck me senseless. I feel his cock swelling inside me and know he is close. He reaches between our sweat slickened bodies and pinches my clit setting off another orgasm that has me seeing stars. I come, screaming his name, he follows after me a second later with my name on his lips.

I have never felt more powerful than I do in this moment, knowing that little old me just brought Rook Murdoch to the highest of highs with my body.

Chapter Nineteen

Rook

Two days later...

Clare has been distant and acting weird since we got back from the tattoo shop the other night. She hasn't let me fuck her and I don't know why. Her pulling away from me has all my doubts creeping in, which is why I called Opal. I now sit in the games room inside Bishop's house with Opal sitting opposite me. She doesn't seem mad that I've blown her off since Clare moved in with me but she does seem worried about what I just told her, which puts me on edge.

"Okay, I'm sensing there is more to this story than you are telling me. From what I know of Clare, she loves you and would do anything for you. I can see it in your eyes and posture that since you and Clare have made your relationship official, that you have overcome a lot of obstacles, which is why I am perplexed as to why she would turn cold suddenly?" I sigh and run a hand down my face.

"She overheard a conversation between me and my siblings and I don't think she likes what she heard." She nods her head, understanding dawning on her.

"Without getting into too much detail, I am assuming that Clare overheard something that most people would balk at?" I reluctantly nod my head. "Have you spoken to her about this *situation*?" I shake my head and she hums her understanding. "I think you and Clare need to have a conversation and be as open and honest with each other as you can." I sigh and slouch into my seat, I was afraid she would say that and honestly, I knew it was coming but I wanted to avoid this topic with Clare. She is the only good thing in my life and I don't want her getting tainted by the darkness in my life. She is way too fucking good for me and I know that. I'm gonna spend the rest of my life waiting for her to wake up and realize she could do better than me.

"What if she can't come to terms with what I have to do?" I ask.

"Will you handling this *situation* help *you*?" I ponder her question for a second before answering.

"I think this will be the final piece of the puzzle that I need to finally move on." Understanding dawns on her, she sits up straighter and crosses her legs as she holds my gaze.

"Then you need to make her see that this is what you need. She knew who you were and where you come from when she decided to establish this relationship with you, Rook. Some things in life aren't always black and white, some areas are gray, and you need to make her see that."

OPAL'S WORDS play over and over in my mind as I make my way back toward to my house, too lost in my own turmoil I don't hear Knight calling out to me until a fucking football hits me in the side of the head. I spin around and pin the motherfucker with a look that promises pain.

"The fuck did you do that for?" I snap. The bastard stands outside King's house with his head held high and his chest puffed up like he's about to do something. I spot all the girls and the kids on the porch behind Knight. It shocks me when I see Clare standing next to Kiara, I thought she would be at home waiting for me.

"So you would pull your head out of your ass!" His words have me clenching my hands into fists at my sides. Clare tries to come to me but Kiara stops her with a shake of her head. Knight eliminates the space between us until there is only a couple inches of space between us. We hold each other's gazes as the tension between us skyrockets to the point where it steals my breath.

"You don't want to do this right now," I grit out through clenched teeth. His eyes darken until nothing but anger can be seen in the depths of his gaze. He steps into me pushing his forehead against mine hard enough that I have to fight not to stumble back a step.

"Oh yeah, I fucking do," he snarls as he shoves me back a step. I fight the flinch that wants to break free from him pushing against my tattoo, but I would never give the fucker that satisfaction.

"You want me to hand you your ass in front of your girl and those twins that could pass as mine?" That snaps his last restraint at the mention of the prospect of me being his kids' father. He launches at me with fists swinging. I allow him to land two shots to the face before a numbness overcomes me and I see nothing but red. My body relaxes and my mind clears as I ready myself to release all the pent-up hate and anger on the one person that I thought had my back *and* front till my dying breath. The day Ivan took me I didn't just lose my freedom, I lost my best fucking friend. I prayed every night that my twin would come for me. I never gave up hope thinking that the bond we shared would ensure that my brother would never give up on me like I would never have given up on him!

I tackle him to the ground, we roll a few times until I manage to end up on top of Knight. I rein blow after blow on him until he eventually bucks me off. He doesn't pause once he's on his feet, charging toward me. Putting all his football training to use for once, he tackles me around the waist, knocking the air from my lungs as I hit the ground. He straddles my legs and punches me continuously. I manage to land a few hits to his face and ribs but the fucker has the upper hand. I hear our names being shouted by someone in the distance but we don't stop—we fucking need this! One minute Knight and I are trading blows, then he's ripped off me and an angry looking Bishop looms above us with Gage and King on either side of him. I hear Knight grunt and peer down to see him sitting on the grass by my legs, so I lash out and boot him right in the face.

"That's enough, Rook!" Bishop shouts. I jump to my feet and get right in the fuckers face before shoving him back a step.

"It'll never be enough!" I scream. Now that I've started, I can't seem to put a lid back on my emotions and they pour out of me. "He fucking left me!" I scream at Bishop as I point toward Knight who is still sitting on the grass cupping his nose. "He fucking left me behind! You all did." Bishop and King both pale at my accusation. Knight clambers to his feet and stumbles over to stand in front Bishop, effectively blocking my view of him until all I can see is a perfect copy of my own eyes and face staring back at me.

"I never fucking left you," he growls, his eyes sparking with an emotion I can't decipher. "I hunted for you every fucking day since the day you disappeared. I never fucking stopped looking for you! Ask all of these fuckers. I refused to hold a wake for you because I never believed you were dead!" He closes the sliver of space between us and rests his forehead against mine but this time it isn't with anger, it's with... regret. "I knew that if you were dead, I would have felt it in my heart. I would never accept the possibility of you ever being dead, Rook, because I can't fucking live without you. If you being alive and hating me for the rest of our lives and ignoring me whenever we see each other is the only way I get to have you in my life, then so be it. I'll take all your anger. I'll take all the fucking blame you need me to take because I hate myself more than you will ever know for not finding you sooner. You're my fucking twin, Rook. Spending eight months without you was the worst and fucking happiest time of my life because I got Koby and my boys but I could never enjoy it because... you weren't here with me to tell me it was okay to love her."

When I see the first tear fall from the corner of his eye every ounce of anger I've had toward him evaporates from inside me. I snake my arm out and grip the back of his neck, pushing my forehead into his harder. He mimics my move. We stand here staring into each other's eyes, finally letting go of all the blame and anger.

"I'll never turn my back on you." The conviction in Knight's tone makes me believe him. "If I could have traded spots with you, I would have. I never gave up, Rook. I swear I didn't. I locked Koby in the bunker and tortured her because I began to believe that you were right and she set you up." My eyes widen in surprise. "I nearly killed her and my sons," he whispers with anguish clear in his tone.

"How?" I say quietly, hyper aware that everyone is looking at us and listening to every word we say, but not caring and needing this moment with my brother.

"She was shot that night at the docks. I didn't care and locked her up. I let her be hit by our guys because I didn't have the guts to do it myself, I had no idea at the time she was pregnant with Havoc and Chaos. I nearly lost all three of them looking for you. She is the only reason I survived without you, Rook. She helped me every fucking day hunt for you. Vin helped as well." He takes a shuddering breath before continuing on. "We all did. None of us gave up hope that you would come back to us. When Gage got a picture of you from Anya, we all knew that the Bratva would burn to the fucking ground for taking you from us. Which is why I am going to help you kill that motherfucker for ever thinking he can come into *our* territory and take you, we are going to make him suffer because when you fuck with one Murdoch, you fuck with all of us!" Tears leak from his eyes and I'm man enough to admit it isn't sweat dripping down my face. I wrap my arms around my twin and crush him against me. He returns my embrace and holds me just as tight as we both stand here and cry for the pain we have been put through at the hands of another.

"I'm so sorry," I say. Knight pulls back and rests his hands atop my shoulders.

"You have nothing to be sorry for."

"I blamed you when none of it was your fault. I made the choice to take Koby to the docks because I thought she was going to drive a wedge between us. My fear of losing you to her ended up with me being taken and really being ripped apart. I needed someone to blame for everything and you were the person I chose. Night after night I fucking prayed you would come and when you didn't, I got angry and bitter not knowing what was going on back here. I'm so fucking sorry for what you went through with Koby. If something had of happened to the twins—"

"Stop!" I clamp my mouth closed at his single word command. "Koby and the boys are fine, we're all fine, Rook. We're gonna be okay, aren't we?" Unable to speak past the lump in my throat, I nod my head and watch as all the tension and uncertainty drains from his eyes and body. I feel Bishop and King shift closer to us, the anger I felt toward the two of them is gone now. I blamed these three because they were here. Car was gone and none the wiser and Gage didn't cop the brunt of my anger because I saw him coming to Russia undercover as him being the only one to care enough to find me. I didn't know that Knight, Bish, King and even Vin came as well.

Chapter Twenty

Sitting around the dinner table with Rook and his family is surreal. There are children present and being loved on by everyone in this family. When I think of what a mob family would look like—this sure as hell isn't it! I mean, for the love of God, I watched Bishop Murdoch, Don to the Murdoch crime family, change his son's diaper today and when I tell you I stood there stunned, I mean I was speechless with my jaw on the floor.

"Clare?" I shake my head and turn to my right to look at Koby. She holds a baby out to me and I stare at the brown haired, coffee-colored eyed baby like he's an alien before looking back to his mother. "Do you mind holding him for a second, I need to change my shirt." I drop my gaze to her shirt and screw my face up at the sight of baby vomit. I reach for the baby boy without even thinking. He smiles at me like I'm the most fascinating thing he has ever seen. All the chatter around me becomes white noise as I stare down at the wee boy in my arms. Longing hits me right in the chest at the thought of me never getting to hold my own baby.

"You okay?" I blink my eyes a couple times and take a deep breath before peering over to my other side at Rook.

"Yeah, just..." I don't know how to express how I'm feeling.

"I know." I frown at him which causes a sad smile to grace his handsome face. He reaches out and brushes his knuckles along his nephew's cheek. "It's hard looking at them," he whispers low enough for only me to hear. "I see me in them and I always wonder what our baby would have looked like." When his eyes meet mine, I see something I haven't seen before... *hope.* "We were robbed of our chance and I just want you to know, I'll spend the rest of my life trying to make what happened right. Or, until you realize your way outta my league and could do so much better than me." Tears spring to my eyes, I don't care that his family is around as I lean forward and seal my lips to his. I know we haven't spoken much in the past two days and I need to find the courage to tell him why I have pulled away, but it's hard.

"Not while you're holding my son!" Knight chastises, causing Rook and I to break a part chuckling. Feeling everyone's gazes on us, my cheeks heat.

"How *did* you two meet?" I dart my gaze to Carlina unsure if I should tell her the truth, or if Rook even wants them to know.

"We met when we were fifteen." Car's eyebrows jump to her hairline at Rook's admission.

"Wait, how?" King asks.

"Luka started hanging with Bish and Clare followed him one night wondering where her brother was sneaking off to. I was out back having a smoke while Tony was rampaging inside and I caught her peeking through the window," Rook says. I fight the smile that wants to break through—the memory of him pinning me against the wall and interrogating me. I think it was in that moment that I knew my heart was done for just from the sight of him.

"You knew this whole time Luka had a sister?" Bishop asks, clearly annoyed he had no idea. Rook just leans his arm on the back of my chair as I bounce the baby on my knee and nods. "You kept that real fucking quiet, didn't you?" Rook and Knight exchange a quick glance, but Bishop the ever observant man that he is catches it. He looks between both his brothers before throwing his hands in the air causing his wife to laugh. "Knight fucking knew about her, didn't he?" Rook rolls his lips over his teeth to keep from smiling and nods.

"Of course, I fucking knew!" Knight says with laughter in his voice. I stare at Rooks twin, taken back that he knew about me. "Who do you think covered for him when he snuck out to meet her?" Bishop looks taken back by this news. I can't stop staring at Knight. When his gaze meets mine, it softens slightly and that throws me off. "I know Rook and I just made up today–" That causes Rook to snort out a laugh beside me. "But I am going to tell you now in front of everyone, I know *everything*." I stiffen in my seat, Rook tenses beside me and pins Knight with a warning glare that he ignores. "You ever run from him again or hurt him like you did before, I promise you I will never stop hunting you. I don't give a fuck who your brother is to mine, I'll show you why we are the most feared family on this side of the US. There is nowhere you can hide from me, Clare, mark my words." I see Rook shift out of the corner of my eye ready to defend me but I beat him to it. I don't need him to fight this battle for me and it's time they all knew the truth and where I stand with Rook.

"You have my word." Knight leans back with a smug look on his face. I'm about to wipe that look off his face in a second. "Just to clarify, you don't know shit!" That has everyone around the table sitting up straight and muttering beneath their breath. I hand the baby to Rook while never taking my angry scowl off Knight, who isn't shy to return my angry look. "The only reason I ran from your brother is because your bastard of a father found out that I was pregnant." I push back from the table and stand, lifting my shirt and push the band of my yoga pants down so he can see the scar his father left, his eyes brows raise as he begins to understand. "Your father made sure my baby would never get a chance to live and he didn't just stop at killing my child. He and a man beat the shit out of me and promised to kill your brother if I didn't leave. So, yes, Knight, I ran but it wasn't because I was selfish. I ran to save your brother's life because I couldn't risk losing him as well as my baby."

As soon as I finish speaking, Kiara hands Royal to his father and dashes around the table to wrap me in her embrace. "I am so fucking sorry that bastard hurt you," she says as she pulls back with tears in her eyes. I smile my thanks as she peers around me to look down at Rook. "That's why you changed." He smiles sadly and nods. "If that cock sucker wasn't dead already, I would fucking murder that son of a bitch for what he put you both through. Everyone comes over to us and gives each of us their sympathy. When it comes time for Knight to stand before me, a hush falls over the room as we each stand here sizing the other up.

"Playboy, you just got good with your twin don't make me have to kick your ass." He rolls his eyes at Koby's threat, causing me to fight back my laughter. Koby is such a badass.

"I had no idea," he says quietly.

"I know, no one knew. Not even Rook." He frowns, then a moment later his brows raise.

"That's why he was pissed when you first came here?" I nod.

"He thought I aborted our baby and ran from him." I feel Rook come up behind me, placing his hands on my hips. I know he stills feels bad about assuming the worst but he doesn't need to. It wasn't his fault.

"I should have known it was more than you breaking his heart. I had no idea you were even pregnant, if I did—" I cut him off when I reach out and grip his hand in mine. I can see from the look in his eyes that he doesn't like to be touched by anyone except Koby but I ignore that fact.

"We don't need to dwell on the past. Rook and I are dealing with it. It's taking time but we'll be okay. I promise to never *intentionally* hurt him. If I do, it won't be hard to find me. I live next door." Everyone laughs at that and we manage to carry on with our meal like nothing happened for a while, until my brother walks in. His gaze finds me immediately and the look of disapproval he shoots me has me standing from my seat. Rook being the beautiful soul that he is stands and covers my back with his body making sure Luka gets the point that I'm *his*.

"Dad would be so disappointed in you." His words having me gasping and slinking back into Rook.

"Shut your fucking mouth!" Rook growls out in warning, everyone around the table tenses. I know none of them will intervene unless Luka oversteps a line. I respect them all so much for that.

"You think me disappearing from your life was an accident?" Luka doesn't give me a chance to answer. "I did that so you wouldn't get caught up in this fucking life. Little did I know you were screwing the son–excuse me that one is now dead so I'll rephrase that. You were screwing the *brother* of my boss. You running was the best thing, you were out of here and safe, but then you had to come back!" Tears cloud my vision at my brother's declaration. "I never wanted you to be a part of this life. Why do you think I was trying to push you out and to move?" I shake my head denying him. "Don't deny it Clare, you are far from stupid." Rooks grip on me tightens.

"Watch it!" he snarls. My brother snaps his gaze to Rook and scoffs in disgust.

"You should have left her be! I warned you to stay the fuck away from her when she ran!" My jaw drops, I spin around and stare up at Rook who has a guilty look on his face.

"Luka knew about me and you?" He grinds his teeth so hard I fear he may break them. He nods stiffly.

"Did you really think he wasn't keeping tabs on you while you were in Oklahoma?" Luka taunts, I can't look away from Rook feeling so betrayed by his lies. "He knew where you were this whole fucking time, Clare. *He* never came after you. I made sure he stayed away so you wouldn't be caught up in this fucking life!" I decide to deal with Rook's betrayal later and turn back to face my brother, pinning him with what I hope is a look that conveys every ounce of anger I feel right now.

"You don't get to stand there and judge me!" I shout. Ally and the other girls grabs the kids and leave the room, wise choice ladies. "You had no fucking right to interfere in my relationship!"

"I had every fucking right!" he shouts back. The guys stand from their seats in warning, but Luka and I ignore them.

"No you didn't—"

"After what Tony did—" Luka's eyes widen and my mouth drops open in shock. I feel Rook press up against my back.

"Who. The. Fuck. Told. You?" Luka darts his gaze between me and Rook. A sob tears out of me, I know my brother and I know that fucking look!

"What did you do?" I cry out, his eyes lower and his shoulders hunch. "What the fuck did you do?" I scream. I can feel the guys confused gazes on me but I don't care. Luka rushes around the table toward me, but Rook steps in front of me blocking me from him.

"She's my sister!" Luka grits out.

"She isn't your anything, she's *mine*." Rook's words just piss me off further, he lies to me and thinks he can stand there and claim me? Yeah, no! I push past him until I am wedged between him and my brother. Luka lowers his gaze to mine and the anguish I see in his eyes has me stiffening as I wait for him to shatter my fucking heart.

"I got caught tracking Kiara for Bishop." My hand flies up to cover my mouth. "I'm so fucking sorry, Clare. I swear I never fucking meant for this to happen. You have to believe me." When he reaches out for me, I dart away from him, hurt covers his features but I don't care.

"What the fuck does my wife have to do with this?" Bishop demands, Luka doesn't take his eyes off me as he answers his boss. I beg him with my eyes to not say it aloud and make it real because I don't think I will ever be able to look at him again if he does.

"Tony caught me tracking Kiara for you. In order to

keep her safe so he wouldn't find her, I lied. He knew I was lying but I didn't think he knew about Clare because I never told anyone about her. Then one night two weeks after he caught me, my dad calls me in a panic and crying." I gasp, my dad called him and I had no idea! "He told me Clare was jumped and in the hospital. He told me she... lost the baby. I knew in that moment that she wasn't jumped. Tony was sending me a warning for covering for you." Tears fall freely down my cheeks. "I helped dad get you out of the state—"

"Motherfucker!" Rook roars before he launches at my brother and they fall to the ground with fists flying through the air. Luka doesn't fight back, just tries to block as many of Rook's hits as he can before Vin and King pull Rook off of him. I can't stand to be around them any longer. I take off and ignore the girls calling after me as I pass by the living room, and run straight out the door. I don't stop running until I reach Rook's house. I fly through the door and straight upstairs to *our* room. Yeah, we now share a room but not for long. I grab Bob off the bed and place him gently into his travel crate before dashing into the walk-in closet and pull a duffle bag from the top, shoving all my clothes inside it—albeit it's not much but still, it's all I have. I clear my stuff from the bathroom and place it all in the bag before I swing it over my shoulder. I make sure not to take any of the clothes Rook bought me. I grab Bob and make my way downstairs, drop the phone he bought me on the couch before racing out the door and out of his life, again.

Chapter Twenty-One

"Stay the fuck away from my sister!" Luka shouts. I fight Vin and King's hold trying to go for him again. Bishop and Knight hold Luka back.

"Fuck you! You fucking got my kid killed." His eyes slam closed as guilt washes over him. "You don't get to fucking close your eyes like a coward, look at me, you fucking pussy!" He does as he's told and holds my gaze. When I see nothing but self-loathing and hatred in his gaze, something inside me tells me to stop. I take deep calming breaths trying to reign in my temper. I can't blame him completely, even though I want to. I should have gone to Bishop the moment I found out Clare was pregnant, he could have helped us. Instead, I thought I could handle this shit on my own. If I'm honest, I'm angrier at myself than

Luka. "You think because you told her that I knew where she was that she would hate me?"

"One can only hope," he mutters beneath his breath.

"Why the fuck didn't you tell me, Luka? That was my baby, *my* fucking kid and the love of my life." His eyes narrow to slits but I push on. "I fucking love your sister, Luka. She is my first love and she *will* be my last whether you like it or not. She will be part of this family. You can either accept that or walk the fuck out that door and wait for someone to put a bullet in your fucking head because you know the only way out is in a box!"

"I never wanted her to be a part of this life. Clare is too good for this world, Rook, you have to know that. I thought by staying away from her and my dad would keep her safe from Tony. After he died, I could have reached out to them but I didn't because they would want to be a part of my life. I'm too far into this world now, our enemies would use her as a way to get to me so I would sell Bishop out." What he says resonates with me and I get his reasoning but I still can't let go of him not telling me about Tony.

"How'd you know it was Tony that hurt Clare?" He shakes his head.

"I didn't, not for sure until she turned up here and saw you again. I saw it in her eyes, she never would have run from you if someone didn't threaten your life. I know my sister, Rook. It broke her to leave you, for you to think the worst of her it killed her. She has no idea that dad and I talked weekly until you went missing. I broke all contact in fear that whoever took you would track down my family. I'm sorry about the baby, I really am, but you need to understand that my sister was my first priority and ensuring she was safe from Tony meant her being away from you and *me*." I hate to admit it but he makes sense and

I respect that. "Clare won't tolerate you killing people, she is good and loves everyone. Fuck." He scrubs a hand down his face. "Do you know how hard it was to tell my own sister she had to move out when I know she can't afford rent?"

"She has a place, with *me*!" I defend. "You did what you could to get her away from our father and try to keep her safe but she still found her way back to me. I won't let her go a second time, Luka, I can't."

"Where the hell is Clare?" Gage interjects, I spin around and scan the room, she isn't here. Luka and I both race out of the room and into the living room thinking she is with the girls.

"Where's Clare?" I demand.

"She ran out of here. We tried to stop her—" I don't wait around for Kiara to finish, I run from the house heading straight for mine. I can hear Luka following after me. I shove the front door open and race up the stairs calling her name. I head straight for our room, checking our bathroom and that's when I notice the sink bare of her things. I head for the wardrobe next, some of her clothes are gone and that's when it hits me, Bob never barked when I came in the room. I look to where his crate normally sits and see his travel crate is gone. I race back down the stairs and find Luka in the living room with her phone in his hand.

"She's gone," he mutters. I stalk over to him and snatch her phone from his hand and race out of the house.

"Not for long," I mutter beneath my breath.

IT'S NEARLY midnight and still no sign of Clare. My brother's, Vin, Luka and our men are scouring the city for her. I have tried everywhere and I'm running out of fucking ideas of where to look.

"Hang a right here," Luka shouts. Knight does as he told and follows Luka's direction until my surroundings become clear.

"The shelter," I breath out, pissed at myself for not thinking of this place. Luka turns to face me.

"I know I am going to be in shit for what happened tonight with Bishop—"

"No, you won't be," I say, cutting in.

"Yeah, I will. This is the second time you and I have gone at it and I was lucky enough to get away with it the first time." Knight and Vin remain silent in the front of the car. "Look after my sister, Rook. Love her like she deserves and make sure she never gets hurt by this life. My biggest fear was always worrying that my involvement with this life would dim the light in her eyes. Don't ever let that light dim."

"I swear it." I hold his gaze so he knows he I am serious as I say, "I'll make sure nothing happens to you, Luka. Out of everyone, Bishop knows what it's like to deal with someone banging his little sister." I ignore Vin's chuckle from the front. "You don't fall under the same category as the other men in his fold. Your sister is going to be a Murdoch and you and I are going to fight from time to time, and your boss is gonna keep his nose out of it." We come to a stop outside of the shelter. I grip the hand ready to go in search of my girl but Luka's grip on my arm stops me.

"One, thank you. Two, let me go after her, Rook. I should have gone after her years ago." I open my mouth to argue but he quickly continues. "She needs to yell at me and hate me. I'll tell her you were here."

"*Are* here," I correct.

"Nah, bro, you need to leave and deal with your Ivan problem now. Finish that shit so when you come for her, there will be nothing in the way of you two." He offers me his hand to shake. I stare at it for a beat before cautiously placing mine in his. "For what it's worth, I'm really sorry about everything you have gone through and for any part I played in keeping my sister from you. You're a good kid, Rook, but I need you to know something."

"What?" I hedge. I feel Vin and Knight's gazes on us but don't pay them any mind as I focus on Luka.

"No one will ever be good enough for her in my eyes. I don't care if your family is rich as fuck and can give her everything she ever wants. I will never willingly walk her down the aisle—" I narrow my eyes to slits in warning. "But, I also won't stand in the way of her happiness. If you make her happy then I guess... I need to let her go." He releases my hand and reaches for the door handle to get out.

"How do you know she's here?" Knight asks, he peers over his shoulder and shoot me a devilish smirk.

"I knew she was here the whole time." I growl, pissed the fuck off at the bastard again in a short span of time. "She needed time to cool off. If we had of come here first, she would have ripped both our balls off. Go handle your shit, Rook, and get right before you come for her," he says, then slams his door closed and heads for the back entry into the shelter.

"What's the play here, brother?" I mull over what Luka said for a minute. He's right. I need to end shit with Ivan and bury my past tonight so I can move forward and not allow it to drag me down or get in the way of mine and Clare's future.

"Take me to Ivan. This shit ends tonight," I grit out and

pray to God I can stomach seeing the fucker that tried to ruin me.

———

THE MOMENT THE CAR STOPS, I'm leaping out and staring at the building in front of me with so many mixed emotions. I turn to look at Knight when he rounds the front of the car, he at least has the fucking decency to look sheepish.

"Bishop made us all swear not to tell you." He tries to plead with me, I shake my head letting him know without words that I am not fucking impressed.

"Be honest, if you knew where he was, you would have fixated on that fact and it would have fucked with your head." I want to deny what Vin says, I can't though. He's right. Knowing Ivan was being held *here* would have wreaked havoc on my mind daily and knowing he was this close to me, would have sent me into a tailspin.

"Ya'll should have told me." My argument is weak, everyone knows it. Two sets of headlights pulling into the carpark has me looking back to Knight.

"Vin text him, he's our brother but he's still the boss." I can tell Knight is weary of how I will react so I put him at ease.

"I know. I knew one of you would have told him and I'm not mad." Knight visibly relaxes. He and Vin come to stand beside me as we watch Bishop, Gage and King climb out of Bishop's Tesla. Knight's Dodge parks beside Bish—Koby, Anya and Ally all climb out. Allison smiles at me and I'll admit, it means a lot to know she is here for me even though I have been distant and frankly a dick to her since I came back. The six of them make their way over to us. Ally being the mother she is doesn't when the others do. She comes for me and I don't hesitate to open my arms for her, a sob tears from her as she runs for me. I wrap my arms around her and hold her close to me as she buries her face in my chest and cries. I feel like an utter dick for how I have treated her these past few months and vow to make it up to her.

"I've missed you so much." She hiccups and I bury my face in the crook of her neck.

"I've missed you to. I promise I'll make it up to you and Meelz." She pulls back and I wipe her tears away with my thumbs. She reaches up and grips my forearms.

"We'd like that very much. She has missed her Uncle Cook a lot." I smile wide at my niece's name for me. Amelia still can't say mine and Knight's names so she calls us Right and Cook.

"Are you sure you're ready for this?" Bishop asks, the no nonsense tone of his voice tells me he's in Don mode. I wrap my arm around Ally's shoulders and tuck her into my side as I meet Bishop's gaze and nod. I turn to King next to see him smiling at us. I'm proud of him for getting over his hang ups and always accusing Ally of cheating on him with one of us. "I need the words, Rook."

Taking a deep breath, I look around me and a sense of rightfulness flows through me. In the pits of my dispare I failed to notice or even care to see that each of these people has always been here for me and only want what's best for me.

"Yeah, B, I'm ready to end this shit and exact my fucking pound of flesh." A dark glint enters Bishop's gaze as he smiles darkly and nods his approval as he leads us inside the gym I now own and run. The place I have been training daily, never knowing that the star of my nightmares was being held just below me.

Chapter Twenty-Two

Clare

I'm huddled up on the threadbare couch in the staff room trying to get comfy and warm with Bob tucked into my chest. I hate bringing him here with me to work, the poor thing always shakes and assumes I am going to leave him behind. I stroke his fur and murmur words of love and reassurance. I've spent the better part of the night bawling my eyes out and now that I have finally stopped, I'm trying to get some sleep before work tomorrow. I can't shut my mind off! I feel so hurt that Rook knew where I was and never had the balls to come and face me. I dealt with the loss of our baby alone. I had no one to turn to. My dad and brother lied to me! Did I do something in a past life to warrant everyone I love shitting on me?

Tears begin to fall again and I don't bother to wipe them away, I'm alone in this world with nowhere to go. I'm sleeping on the couch in an animal shelter. The universe is having a great big laugh at my expense right now. I may as well set myself up in one of the cages with the dogs and hope a family will come along and adopt me. Bob sitting upright and barking snaps me out of my turmoil. I sit up and try to calm him, not wanting to be caught by one of the staff that may have come in to retrieve something they forgot. I feel panic rising inside me as I hear the sound of footfalls coming toward me. My breaths become shallow rapid pants as I wait to see if whoever it is will come in here and catch me. I can't lose this job! I need the money to live now that I have no place to go.

The door to the staff room opens and Bob goes into hysterics barking. My jaw unhinges when I see who it is standing in the open doorway. When his gaze lands on me, his features slacken and a guilty look enters his gaze. I can't stop the sob that tears out of me. He rushes over and drops down onto the couch beside me, pulling me to him and holding me and a barking Bob while I cry. I'm so confused, I don't know which way is up at this point and I hate that.

"I'm here, Clare-bear, I got you," he says as he holds my sobbing form. We stay like this for so long and Luka doesn't moan or groan, he just sits there and holds me tight lulling me into a false sense of security. Even as a child whenever Luka would tell me everything would be okay or hold me close whenever I was sad, I always knew everything would be okay and we would make it through whatever life threw at us. When he met the Murdoch's, he pulled away from me. I thought I was losing my brother until Rook found me. He took away the ache of my brother being gone so much, until he was ripped away from me as well and I was left on my own to care for my sick Dad. Losing Dad was fucking hard, he was all I had. Coming to New York again after Luka pushed me away that first time was hard, but I had nowhere else to go and I didn't think any of this would happen. I thought Rook would be away at college so I wouldn't run into him. I dreamed my brother and I would mourn the loss of our dad together and spend the weekends hanging out watching movies and catching up on all the time that we lost.

"I'm sorry for being a burden," I mumble against his chest. He sighs and rests his chin on top of my head.

"You're not a burden. I am so fucking sorry for making you feel like you are. You're my little sister and I'll always be here for you."

"Then why did you turn me away when I first came to tell you about Dad?" He pushes me back and cups my cheeks between his large hands. I gasps when I see the remnants of tears on his cheeks.

"Because I never wanted you tainted by this life that I chose to live."

"Then leave it, don't go back!" I beg. He smiles sadly and I know no matter what I say he will never do as I asked.

"If Rook walked in here right now and poured his heart out to you, would you tell him to fuck off?" I bite my lip and shake my head, he got me there. "This life is hard and dangerous—"

"Then why do you do it?"

"Because they are good people," he answers, but I can tell there is more to this story so I push him.

"How did you get into this life?" He releases his hold on me and slouches back into the couch. I tuck my legs under me and pull Bob into my lap as I wait for Luka to speak.

"Tony Murdoch was the one who found me." My mouth opens in shock. "He found out I was kicked out from my last two high schools for hacking. When he learned at the age of seventeen that I got pinged for hacking into the octagon for fun and was the youngest person to ever make the FBI's most wanted list, he recruited me." I remember that when he got kicked out of school Dad and Lilly were so mad. "It took me three months after working for him to realize he was a piece of shit. I wanted out and Bishop told me if I helped him take down his father and transfer all the accounts and business holdings to him, he would grant me my freedom."

"His father is dead now, so why did you stay?" He rests his head back against the couch and closes his eyes.

"I couldn't come back, I was in too deep and Dad had no idea I was a wanted man. I didn't want to bring that type of heat to you or him, so Bishop offered me a job and I took it. Why do you think I could never fly to OKC? I would have been flagged at the airport and thrown in jail for the rest of my life. There is a reason why I don't travel commercial, Clare."

"But you went to Russia and Miami," I protest. He lulls his head to the side and pins me with a *are you stupid* look.

"I flew on Bishop's private jet. Every time I leave the country it's a risk, but it's one I'm willing to take after everything Bish has done for me."

"What has he done for you?" I can't disguise the anger in my voice.

"He gave me a chance to be more than I was. I was a dumb kid who got caught and would have ended up in prison for hacking. B gave me a place where I belonged. They aren't just my bosses, they are my friends." I snort, he's out of his mind if he thinks that. "It may not seem like it but they are. I would go to war for each of them. King is my best friend and has asked me to be his daughter's godfather. I'm sorry I left you, Clare, but I had to do this. I never felt like I belonged but being with this family I finally feel like I do, ya know?" All the air drains from my lungs, I know exactly what he means.

"I get it. Rook has this way of making me feel like I don't need a place to call home, I just need him. Don't get me wrong, I'm mad at you and him for lying to me but I kind of get it. If I had of known—"

"You would have tried to stop me?" I nod and he laughs but there is no humor to it. "You couldn't have stopped me. I needed to do this. My only regret is that you were dragged into this, all I ever wanted was to keep you safe, Clare. I'm sorry I wasn't there for you and Dad when you needed me most. And I'm so fucking sorry you went through losing Dad on your own." The lump forms in my throat again as I fight back tears.

"It's okay," I choke out.

"No, it isn't. I should have been there for you both. I tried to pay Dad's medical bills the other day only to find out that Rook Murdoch already took care of it." A thought hits me and I gasp as I reach for his hand and clasp it in mine.

"Him paying the bill, does that mean you will have to work for them or do something bad because of that?" This time when he laughs there is humor to it, and I scowl at him as I wait for his laughter to die off.

"No. Rook doesn't do anything he doesn't want to, and believe me the money he paid is nothing to them. They own New York, Clare. Soon, Bishop will take over Miami from Anthony Bennett and one day his son will run it as well. They are the first family in history to ever rule over two separate cities. Bish is ambitious and won't stop until his family runs the whole of the US."

"I don't understand."

"Bishop, King, Knight, Gage, Rook and even Carlina never loved anyone, not even their own parents, only each other. Except everything changed and Bishop wasn't willing to settle anymore when he got Kiara back. It drove him to want to ensure her safety. King fell in love and it made him want to help Bishop more to ensure the safety of his daughter. Same goes for Knight, Rook, Gage and Car. Well, Vincent will never allow anything to happen to his wife."

"Why?" I ask, a look of respect overcomes Luka's features.

"Bishop, Gage, King and Knight all changed because they fell in love. They will not stop until they rule this country and ensure the safety of their wives and children. But, Carlina ran from her brothers wanting her freedom only to be kidnapped by Vincent." I gasp and wait for him to continue. "Carlina fell in love with the number one assassin in the world. Vincent is known as the *Bloodhound*. He can track any person, anywhere and never misses a kill shot until Carlina." Warmth spreads through me at hearing their love story. "No one will ever get close enough to Car to ever touch her and because of that, her brothers have accepted Vincent as family. This family is loyal to a fault and now, their baby brother has gone and fallen in love."

I shake my head denying his claim. "He doesn't love me. If he did, he wouldn't have lied and kept his distance." Luka squeezes my hand and shakes his head.

"Rook has been in love with you for years, Clare. When you ran with Dad you didn't see him. He changed, he went from being carefree and drunk on life to this shell of a man that hid behind his humor and football. You know why he pushed so hard to excel in football even though his father hated it?" I shake my head. "He did that because he thought if he got drafted he would finally be good enough for you. He had always planned to come for you, Clare-bear, you just beat him to the punch." My eyes fill with tears.

"I-I can't, Luka. I love him, I've always loved him, but I can't sit by and watch as he kills people."

"Then let him go, Clare, walk away now and never come back. I'll give you the money you need but you can never return to the US or make contact with me. He let you go once and I can tell you now, he won't let you go again without a fight."

I frown at him. "What are you saying?"

"You want out of this life and away from Rook, then now is your *only* chance while he deals with his past. You want to leave, I'll get you a new identity but you need to go far away. Go to New Zealand and start a life there but you can never come back and you will never be Clare Santiago again."

"You would do that for me?" I ask. He smiles sadly as he wraps his arm around my shoulders and pulls me into his side.

"If I believed it's what you really wanted, yes." I tense beside him. "But you and I both know that you won't go because when you love someone you never give up on them. Look at me, I treated you like shit and you still love me. Rook's father hurt you and still you never blamed Rook for that."

"What do I do?" I whisper.

"Rook was drowning before you came back. He never spoke to anyone when he came back, until you broke into the house and he saw you. You've brought him back from the brink of no return, Clare. You run, you will destroy him and believe me, if you do that, it won't just be Rook hunting you. His siblings and fuck even the girls would hunt you down. The guys may seem scary but believe me they're a fucking picnic compared to their girls, they are fucking crazy." We both chuckle at that. I can tell they are bad bitches and would never allow anyone to hurt their family.

"What do I do then? I'm not like the others, Luka. I can't go around hurting people." His hold on me tightens.

"They don't go around killing people, Clare, they only do it if they have to. Like, Bishop and the others stopped the biggest sex trade operation in the world and rescued Rook at the same time. Bish is working with the Bratva and both of them together are making sure no one tries to start up another skin trade. Anya owns and runs shelters in Russia for women. Koby and Ally are opening some here in the US. They may do fucked-up things but they balance it out with the good. Rook has to do this, he is only doing this—"

"Because of the deadline," I cut in, sounding bitter even to my own ears.

"No. Rook is doing this so he can finally let go of his past and not allow it to keep dragging him down. He is doing this for *you*, Clare." I pull away from him and search his gaze for a meaning but can't find one.

"Why would he do this for *me*?"

"Because he wants to heal and be good for you. Rook went through hell at the hands of Ivan. He doesn't know any other way, Clare. This is who he is, who he was born to be." I mull over his words for a while. Can I be with him even though I know what he does while he isn't with me?

"Do they hurt innocent people?"

"No, they aren't like their father. They save people, Clare, and that is why the other families all over the US are going to come for them, because they don't rule over people and hurt them. I mean, they do hurt people, but not innocent ones."

"Why are you telling me all of this?" He smiles and that smile throws me off kilter.

"You and I both know you already made your choice ten minutes ago. You will be a part of this family, you just need to accept it now because your boy needs you." I furrow my brow confused at his meaning. "Rook is facing his worst fears right now, sis. He may have his family surrounding him but there is one person he wants more than anyone by his side as he does this. He needs *you*." My heart beats faster in my chest as I picture the love of my life scared and putting on a brave face for the sake of his family.

"I need to go to him," I say as I climb to my feet and place Bob in his travel crate, then face my brother as he slowly stands and smiles proudly down at me.

"Dad would be so fucking proud of you, Clare. You're strong like Mom but you're smart like Dad." I rush him and wrap my arms around his waist, holding him tight. He returns my hug and places a kiss to the top of my head. "I'll never say he is good for you but I will say he is trying to be good enough for you, Clare, and that right there, earns him my respect." He untangles himself from me and peers down at me with a serious look in his eyes. "Mafia family or not, if Rook ever hurts you, I will fucking kill him with my bare hands." It shouldn't but his words bring a watery smile to my face.

"I love you, brother."

"I love you too, little sister. Now, let's go get your boy, then I can get my beating over with." I tap him as he reaches for my bag and Bob's crate.

"What the hell do you mean *beating*?" He cringes.

"I laid hands on one of the Don's brother's, I have to answer for that—"

"You leave Bishop to me, no one is going to fuck with my brother!" I snarl, causing Luka to throw his head back and laugh.

"Ah, sister, there is no way you will ever be *Ruined By The Rook* with that attitude."

Chapter Twenty-Three

Rook

We all follow Bishop down to the basement of the gym. I start to feel like my skin is crawling the closer we get to where Ivan is being held. Honestly, I didn't even know the gym had this beneath it, though it makes sense now why Gage hasn't done the full changeover of the gym. They didn't want me to have full reign of the place and stumble upon Ivan. We near the end of the corridor and I spot Sally. He's a big fucker and the guy Bish normally uses to collect our *debts*. At the sight of all of us, he turns and unlocks the door, then pushes it open. Everyone walks in but my legs won't work. I'm stuck, rooted to the spot. I close my eyes and will myself to take the final steps and end this. I need to close this chapter of my life so I can finally be free to go after my girl.

"We're here with you, always." I open my eyes to find Bish standing in front of me. For once he doesn't have his mask in place, he is letting me see everything he is feeling—love, hate, pity, compassion for me. "I don't tell any of you this, well I don't say it ever, but I do what I do for this family because I love each and every one of you, Rook." That has my eyes widening and my brows jumping into my hairline. "If I could go back in time and take your place, I would fucking do it in a heartbeat because I hate seeing the look of fear in your eyes at the mention of this cunt!"

"Bishop–" I try to cut in but he won't let me.

"No, I need to say this." He places his hand on my shoulder and holds my stare. "You're my baby brother, Rook, and I should have protected you. I failed you and I will never forgive myself for that. He can never hurt you again, brother. I will never fucking allow that bastard to ever go free. He is on borrowed time and it's time for you to get your retribution on the son of a bitch." His words spur something to life inside me. It feels a lot like strength, strength I didn't even know I possessed until now. When I give him a curt nod, he returns the gestures and turns to Sally. "Get the camera and get back here ready to record."

"Yes, sir," he says as he races off to do as Bish ordered. When Bish turns and heads back into the room, I give myself a second. I place my hand over my heart and rub at the tattoo that I got there. I know she hasn't seen it yet but I didn't get it for her, I got it for *me*. Taking a deep breath, I square my shoulders and hold my head high as I stalk into the room with the swagger of a cocky motherfucker. At the sight of me, the others part and reveal Ivan Volkov. I fight the panic that rises inside me at the sight of the old cunt. He wears a shirt but it's torn and looks more like tattered rags. He has no pants on and is curled into a ball in the corner of the room. When he turns his head and spots me, recognition shines in his eyes and they widen slightly. The sight of hope in his green eyes that I will save him has me clenching my fists at my sides.

"Who's the dvornyaga (*mutt*) now, suka (bitch)?" I growl in a voice that doesn't sound like my own. Ivan flinches and huddles further into the corner. The sight of him cowering, beaten and bloody should make me feel empowered but I can't seem to find it within myself to pull on the strength I felt mere seconds ago. As if sensing my turmoil, King steps forward and grips a hand full of Ivan hair and yanks him forward until he is on his knees staring up at me with a defeated look in his eyes, a look I know too fucking well.

"Ivan over here has been *played* with well by Sally and his boys. Isn't that right, Sal?" King says as Sally enters the room carrying a camera and tripod with three other guys behind him. He blows Ivan a kiss, causing the Russian to recoil in fear.

"Sure have, boss. My cock's getting hard at the thought of taking him for another round." I keep the shocked look off my face. King chuckles darkly, Ally walks up beside her man and smiles at me, her eyes are full of bloodlust.

"You see, Sally here has a kink and Bish and King can't allow said kink out into the world." I quirk a brow in question as Ally slips around King to stand on the other side of Ivan. He flinches away from her, telling me that both Ally and King have been down here before. "Sally loves to fuck unwilling participants. Ivan fought valiantly for a while and all it did was fuel Sal to force him into submission. Once the fight left him, and he became willing, Sal was over it so he handed him off to at least a few dozen others and now Ivan can't seem to sit. Lord only knows why." The humor in her tone has me reeling. Ally looks like a fucking school teacher, yet she stands in front of me talking about torture like Lucifer's bride.

"Needless to say, Ivan has been warmed up for you," Gage supplies. Anya moves around the others to stand beside me. At the sight of her a fire enters Ivan's gaze.

"Predatel (*Traitor*)," Ivan spits at Anya. Gage doesn't hesitate, stepping forward and punching him right in the face.

"You ever fucking speak to her again and I'll cut your fucking tongue out, you worthless piece of shit!" Anya swoons at Gage's show of protectiveness over her.

"He is not the star of your nightmares anymore, you're the star of his. You will live a life of wonder, love and happiness and he will never get that. The last thing he will see before he meets his maker is your face. You will be the last thing he sees before he leaves this world!" Her words have me standing taller. I turn to Sally and rattle off a list of items I need. No one says anything as he disappears from the room. I look to the other three and tell them what I need from them, they all nod and scurry from the room to do as I asked.

I bend down so Ivan and I are eye level, the defeated look in his eyes is now gone and replaced by hate–good. "I'm going to make you wish you never took your first breath." I make sure he can see in my eyes that I am not broken, I am strong. I'm standing right here strong, surrounded by loved ones, while he is here all alone and at the mercy of *me*.

"You tried with all your might to destroy me. You thought you succeeded but I'm here to tell you, you nearly did until someone I never thought I would see again appeared in my life at the exact time I needed her." I can see the confusion on his face. I'm not saying this for his benefit, I'm saying it for mine. "You will die here tonight but before I deliver that final blow, you are going to fucking suffer, you are going to wish you left me to die that night at the docks."

WHEN SAL and the others return with what I asked for, I task them with strapping Ivan down to the table they brought in. He tries to fight but it's no use. Once he is strapped down, they step away. The sight of his flaccid cock has bile rushing up my throat and I have to swallow a few times to keep it down. I hate that I know what that cock feels like inside me and what it tastes like! Sally pushes the cart over to the side of the table and I smirk at the sight of the ice bucket with the white cloth over it, shit is about to get real.

At my approach he fights against his restraints but it's futile, he'll never break free. Bish, King, Knight, Gage and Vin stand on the opposite side of the room. Koby stands in front of Knight with his arms wrapped around her. Anya has the same position as her but not Ally, she stands beside King clutching his arm with a smile on her face. I nod to Bishop, letting him know to set up the feed. He and Vin set up the tripod, setting the camera up so Andreas and the others can watch live. Vin steps away and sets up a laptop. Within seconds, Andreas' face fills the screen and a gleeful smile stretches across his face.

"Andreas, as promised, Ivan Volkov," Bishop says.

"Russia thanks you for this," he says in answer before Andreas turns his gaze to me. "I hope you get everything you need from this moment. I apologize for the rush but as you can imagine I have citizens here that he and his family have hurt and they are screaming for his death." I don't bother with words, just nod and turn back to Ivan. His eyes are wide with fright. Knowing our rolls are reversed, and he's the one who is terrified of me, makes me feels strong and superior.

"I'm going to make sure that your last hours are spent writhing in agony. I want you to feel every fucking thing I do to you, which is why I have shots of Adrenalin here to keep you awake through this whole procedure."

"You are fucking nothing. I destroyed you and it was fucking glorious!" he shouts. I spy the others shift ready to come to my aide if I need it but I don't. I pat Ivan on the chest in the most condescending way.

"You keep telling yourself that, *dvornyaga*, but let's get one thing clear here, shall we? You never fucked me, I fucked you and that right there means I was the one with power, not you. I hope you have a condom for your heart because I'm about to fuck the shit out of your feeling's, cunt." I ignore his tirade of insults as I start to whistle and pull the white cloth off the bucket and grab the rat out, at the sight of the rat Ivan begins to thrash even harder. "King, Bish come hold him still. Knight, come get the bucket." They do as I ask. I place the rat on his stomach and Knight slams the bucket on top of the rat with enough force to knock the wind out of Ivan.

I turn back to the cart and decide to trade the blow torch in for some pliers and call Gage over to hold his head steady. I don't warn him or even tell him what I'm doing, I just start ripping his fucking teeth out, one by one. His screams turn to gurgles as blood begins to fill his mouth. I'm not a complete asshole, I leave his two front behind and smile down at him when I'm finished.

"There you go, now you look much better, *Bugs.*" I can't make out what the fuck he is saying so I decide to grab the blow torch. I call Vin over, the table is fucking crowded but it feels great knowing that Ivan is surrounded and scared shitless. I hand Vin the pliers and tell him what I need him to do. He doesn't balk, just wrenches his mouth open and grips Ivan's tongue with the pliers as I flick the blow torch on. Ivan begins to scream and tries harder to get free but it's no use. I hold the torch over his tongue, his screams of pain are like music to my ears. Two minutes into burning his tongue off and the fucker has the cheek to pass out! "Someone give him a shot and wake his ass up!"

"On it!" Ally calls as she races over and grabs the syringe off the cart, pushes between Vin and Bish and stabs it right into his heart then pushes the plunger. Ivan comes to within a few seconds, screaming, so I go back to work. Once there is a nice little hole in his tongue, I move onto my friend in the bucket. I hand Knight the Miller's welding gloves to slip on so he doesn't get burnt holding the bucket for me. Bish and the others step back.

"You ready?" I ask my twin. He shoots me a dark smirk and nods. Ivan lifts his head and tries to hurl what I am sure is insults but we can't understand a fucking word of it. To shut him the fuck up I put the blow torch over his cock and relish at the screams that tear from him as I burn his fucking cock off! "Fuck!" I growl out when he passes out again. I turn back to the cart to grab a syringe but pause when I see Clare samanding in the doorway with Luka at her back. Her gaze is glued to Ivan. I'm fucking frozen in place at the sight of her *here* where *he* is! "What the fuck are you doing here?" She jerks back at the harsh tone of my voice. I drop the torch and move toward her but keep a couple feet of space between us. Her eyes search mine and I expect to see revulsion in her gaze at the sight of me. Instead, all I see is understanding.

"I..." She takes a deep breath and squares her shoulders. I spy Sally out of the corner of my eye moving toward us, I pin him with a look daring him to touch her.

"You lay a finger on her and it's your cock I burn off next!" He nods and steps back against the wall and I focus back on Clare. "Why are you here, sunshine?"

"Because Luka helped me understand some things." I cut a glance at him over her head, he rolls his eyes playfully. "I know you have to do this and I also know we have things to discuss but I can't let you do this on your own unless... you want me to go?" The uncertainty in her voice guts me.

"I always want you with me." A timid smile graces her beautiful face. "But, you are my sunshine and I can't allow you into this darkness."

"But–" I cut her off.

"No. I need to do this and I don't want any part of this touching your goodness, so you can't stay." The crestfallen look on her face has me hating myself. She drops her gaze to her shoes. "Can you wait for me upstairs?" Her eyes snap back to mine and she eagerly nods.

"Y-yeah, I can do that." I look to Luka next. "Wait with her, I'll be there soon." He nods and tries to usher her from the room but she breaks free of his hold and launches herself at me wrapping her arms around my neck. I grip her waist as she places a kiss to my lips. "I won't let him take you from me, when this is over I don't want to talk about the past. I want us to start fresh and move on." That has a smile pulling at my lips.

"You got it, baby, now get your ass out of here, Daddy's got work to do," I say as I wiggle my brows drawing a laugh from her. She follows Luka out and I don't pull my gaze from them until they round the corner and I lose sight of them. I turn back to Ivan with a renewed sense of strength. His eyes are hazy, his lids are dropped from the pain. Good. I march over to the cart, grab the blow torch and nod to Knight as I flick it on and begin to heat the bucket. Ivan's eyes snap wide as the rat begins to squeal and claw at his stomach. "You know rats will claw through any surface to escape the heat, my little friend here is going to claw his way through your skin until he reaches your intestines. You'll still be alive the whole way through, until he begins to gnaw on them and eventually you will bleed out and die," I shout over the squeal of the rat and his screams of agony. When I see his eyes begin to roll back, I shoot a look to King.

"Got it," he says as he stabs another round Adrenalin into the cunt's heart. Fucked if I know if you can die from too much adrenalin and honestly, I give zero fucks. I just want this bastard to fucking suffer! Ten minutes go by, his screams are the only sound in the room when his body goes into shock. I know our rat friend has found his way through the skin and is inside him. I turn the torch off allowing the rat to feast and end this cockroach's life. I move up beside his head and hold his stare as he coughs and splutters blood. When his head lulls to the side, I grip his chin and hold it tight keeping his gaze on me.

"Take a good long look at me, it's the last thing you will ever see in this world. Die knowing that you were *Ruined By The Rook*. Just know I will live the rest of my life never thinking about you again. No one will ever remember you existed after this moment and the Volkov name will die with you because Anya will carry on as a Murdoch." He gaze bores into mine as he takes his last breath.

For the first time in months, I feel like I can breathe easier.

Knowing the man who *played* me, *tormented* me, *tortured* me and *tempted* me to take my own life is dead because we *turned* the tables on him—*ruined* him and his brother—has a weight lifting off my shoulders.

Chapter Twenty-Four

Luka and I sit here on one of the bench seats in the gym waiting for Rook to... finish. I feel a sense of rightfulness wash over me. I'm back in the city I grew up in with my brother by my side, my first love back where he belongs, with me. I used to waste time thinking about what type of house I wanted to call home. *Home* isn't a place, it's a person and my person is Rook. I nudge Luka with my shoulder and smile at him.

"Good God, you have that look in your eyes."

"What look?" I abolish.

He points an accusing finger at me. "That look!"

I roll my eyes and shrug. "I have no idea what you are talking about."

"Bullshit, what the hell are you up to?" he accuses.

"Can I not just smile at my brother?" He scoffs and shakes his head.

"No. You forget I know you, and that look in your eyes tells me you are planning something and..." He jumps to his feet with a horrified look on his face. "Oh, that is fucking gross!" he says as he begins to pace the length in front of me before pausing and jabbing that finger in my face again. "I don't ever and I mean fucking ever want to see that or hear that shit come out of your mouth again! Eww." I can't contain my laughter any longer, throwing my head back and letting my laughter loose as tears leak out of the corners of my eyes.

"What's so funny?" At the sound of his husky voice, my laughter dics off and I'm standing within seconds and staring at him. Luka pins Rook with an angry glare.

"You keep... that," he points toward Rook's crotch and I have to bite my lip to keep my laughter in, "away from her. I don't ever want to see that look in her eyes again or hear— fuck. Why couldn't she be a nun!?" Laughter shines in Rook's eyes at Luka's clear unease. In his defense he is right. I was thinking about all the ways Rook could make up him leaving me alone for four years and it did involve him and I being horizontal. Rook closes the space between him and my brother and pats him on the shoulder.

"Sorry, bro, hate to break it to you but if you move in next door you're gonna be hearing your sister scream my name daily." Luka jumps away from Rook's touch like it burnt him. My brother turns and scowls at me. I hold my hands up as if I'm surrendering.

"I swear to God, Clare, if I hear anything, I mean *anything*, I will fucking bury him and lock your ass in a tower somewhere." Rook and I both break out into hysterical laughter. Luka storms off muttering about us being assholes and not wanting to murder his boss's brother. When our laughter finally subsides, we stand here awkwardly just staring at each other for a long time until he finally breaks the silence.

"So…"

I bite the corner of my lip as I scuff the toe of my shoe along the floor. "So…" I reply unsure what to say. He sighs loudly and runs a hand through his hair.

"I don't know what I'm supposed to say. I thought I would have time on the ride while coming to get you after… this to come up with something to say." He chuckles but it's forced.

"I guess me showing up ruined that plan, huh?"

"Yeah." He smiles sheepishly.

"Can I say something?" He nods but looks apprehensive about what I have to say. "We fell head over heels in love and then tragedy struck. We should have been smarter about things and told each other, but we didn't. We lost four years together and I don't want to die with dreams about what it might have been like being with you. I want to die with memories of what it *is* like being loved by you." His eyes spark to life at my words. He doesn't use words, just closes the space between us, cups my cheeks and kisses me until we both break apart panting and gasping for air. Just as I catch my breath, he grabs me again lifting me off the floor. I squeal in surprise as I latch my legs around him and rest my hands on his shoulders. "What are you doing?" I ask as he starts moving toward the other side of the gym.

"Sunshine, I am covered in fuck face's blood. I need a shower but I also need to fuck you so you have that in your *memories*." I scoff.

"And your point is?" I ask as he pushes a door open and

I peer over my shoulder to find he has walked us into an empty locker room.

"I'm going to kill two birds with one stone—shower and fuck you at the same time." His words have me clenching my thighs tighter around his waist and my core pulsing with need.

"What if the others come in?" My argument is weak, he knows it and so do I. He doesn't stop moving until we enter the open shower stalls, places me on my feet and holds my waist.

"You can either strip by yourself or I'll do it for you, those are your only two options." The rasp in his tone tells me he needs this and I am powerless to deny this man anything, so like the good girl I am, I begin to undress. He does the same. When I stand before him, bare and ready for him, his eyes drink me in and send a shiver down my spine. Just as he reaches for me I gasp and place my hand against his chest.

"What is that?" I ask as I stare transfixed on the tattoo that covers his heart. I never noticed it before because his whole upper body is now littered with ink.

"This is so he or she will always be close to my heart. I never got to meet them or know they existed for long but I still loved them." Tears fill my eyes as I stare at the angel wings with the words *Daddy's little baby, you live on through me* in the center "There is something else you should see, he tilts his neck to the side and bends down. Right there between his neck and shoulder it says *Sunshine*. I trace my finger along his pet name for me and sniffle, fighting back the tears. I didn't think I could love him more than I already do, but I was wrong, so fucking wrong! He moves back, grips my waist and lifts me off my feet as I wrap my legs around him. He reaches out and flicks the shower on while keeping us out of the spray as it heats up. "You see, Clare, there is no me without you. You can try to leave me but I'll hunt you down. There is no *I want you to be happy, even if it isn't with me* bullshit. You're mine and I don't care if I have to make you fall in love with me daily for the rest of my life because, sunshine, I have no reason to live if you aren't with me."

I don't answer with words, instead I seal my lips to his and show him with my body that I feel exactly the same way he does. Rook is my beginning, middle and end. He walks us backward until my back is flush against the tiled wall, I gasp at the coldness. He uses that to his advantage and pushes his tongue into my mouth. We fight for dominance through this kiss but in the end, he wins. I submit to him and allow him to lead me, he could lead me into the fiery depths of hell and I would follow willingly. He tears his mouth from mine and captures my nipple in his mouth causing me to arch off the wall and cry out. He switches sides but doesn't suck this one, he bites down on my nipple and scrapes his teeth along the bar in it. I squirm against him trying to grind against his cock.

"Nah uh." Is all he says before he lifts me even higher, drawing a small shout from me when he settles me over his shoulders so his face in right in line with my pussy. All protests die on my tongue when he swipes his own through my slick folds. We both moan at the same time. Rook is fucking gifted at using his tongue, the man needs no help or directions on how to pleasure a woman. When he pushes his tongue inside my tight wet hole I cry out and buck against his face. He grips the globes of my ass, holding me in place, as he devours my pussy until I am screaming his name loud enough to wake the dead downstairs and squirting all over him. He laps at me, bringing me down gently, then pushes his tongue inside me tasting my release. He has my pussy trying to clench his tongue, trying to hold it inside me.

"Rook!" I plead. He finally relents and helps me slide down his front until my legs lock around his waist. I blush slightly, embarrassed when I see my cum dripping down his chin and coating his chest.

"You taste like *sunshine*," he growls out before smashing his lips to mine and forcing his tongue inside until I taste my own release from him. I moan at the taste, I love how I taste on *him*. He slowly pushes his cock inside me, I can't help but clamp down on him, he feels so fucking good inside me. "You like that, baby?" he grits out as he continues to push inside me.

"Yes, I love how you fucking fill me."

"Then take all of me, baby," he growls as he slams the rest of the way inside me, causing us both to cry out. His thrusts are punishing and I know from the grip he has on my waist I'll have bruises tomorrow, but I don't care. I need him to fuck me hard and make me come all over his cock. "Fuck, sunshine, you fit me like a fucking glove."

"Fuck me harder and make me come. I want everyone to hear me scream so they know you're mine!" His eyes blaze with lust at my declaration and possessiveness over him.

"Only yours, baby," he growls before his pace picks up. His cock slams inside my pussy three more times before he hits that glorious G-spot making me scream his fucking name so loud my throat grows hoarse. He pulls out of me only leaving the tip at my entrance and I squirt all over him without a care in the world. Call me crazy, but I love the fact that he is covered in my cum. He places me on my feet and then orders me to my knees. I do as instructed and open my mouth waiting for him to fill it. "You gonna swallow every drop?"

"Yes!" I breath out as he rams his cock inside my mouth.

"Fuck yes, suck it." I do as he says and bob up and down on his cock making sure to swirl my tongue along the underside. I scrape my teeth along his length, causing to shudder. "Take me all the fucking way, baby. I'm gonna come down your throat." I obey him like a puppet and relish the feeling of getting him off when he comes shouting my name as jets of his cum shoot down my throat. I swallow every drop of him, moaning at the taste—he tastes so fucking good. He pulls free of my mouth. Panting and breathless, he helps me to my feet. I smile up at him which earns me a cocky grin. "Let's get cleaned up, then get home so I can spend the whole day fucking memories into you." I swat his chest and laugh at the dork that I am madly in love with.

ROOK MANAGES to find a pair of sweats and a discarded shirt in someone's locker, it beats him wearing his blood-stained clothes from earlier. I brush those thoughts away as I slip my hand into his and he leads us from the locker room.

"Any chance you left the rat at the shelter?" I gasp and smack his arm earn a chuckle from him. "I'll take that as a no."

"You bought said *rat* for me, remember?"

"Yeah, now I'm thinking I should have just wrapped a bow around my dick for you instead of buying you the new star of my nightmares." We both laugh at that as we walk out hand in hand. I freeze at the sight of his family, each wearing the look of laughter as if they know exactly what we were just doing. When my gaze lands on my brother, I cringe and shift closer to Rook who drops my hand and wraps his arm around my shoulders drawing me into his side. He walks us over to the others and I can't help the blush that spreads up my neck and on to my cheeks.

"Just so we're clear, Koby and I were the first to christen that fucking shower block!" I groan and bury my face into Rook's side as everyone breaks out into fits of laughter.

"Fucking Murdoch's!" I hear my brother snap before he stomps out of the gym.

"He'll come around." Bishop's voice has me shifting my gaze to him. The man is scary as fuck but if I want to last in this family, I need to woman up and show him I can be a badass too, kind of, sort of, maybe the jury is still out on that one.

"Please don't hurt my brother." Bishop's brows raise, silence ensues at my words and I feel everyone's eyes on me.

"Now, why would I do that?" His smug tone only serves to irritate me.

"Because I am asking you not to. Luka and Rook are going to butt heads and no offense, I know you are the boss and all that, but it's none of your business when they have spats over me." When his eyes narrow I gulp and mentally facepalm myself when I come back to reality and realize what I just did and who the hell I am speaking to.

"You got balls, girl. You may just make it in this dick thriving family after all." Koby's words have some of the tension easing from my body, but I'm not stupid enough to believe just because the girls like me that Bishop will go easy on me.

"Tell ya what, you stick around and keep my brother happy and I may just let your brother live." I suck a breath in at his words, but I can't take that, I need more from him.

"I can do that but I need your word that Luka won't be

harmed. If he is or if anything happens to him being Rook's brother won't save you from me." He steps in closer. Rook's hold on me tightens, I crane my neck back to stare up at him and make sure to keep my mask of indifference in place.

"Are you threatening me?"

"No, I'm just giving you a friendly warning is all," I reply with a sweet smile.

"Oh, fuck me dead, Kiara has already corrupted her!" Gage shouts before laughing. Bishop growls and mumbles about his wife needing to be taught a lesson, then storms from the room. All of us laugh at his expense.

I think I'm going to fit in just fine after all.

Chapter Twenty-Five

Rook

Six months later...

I stand behind Clare and Luka and watch as they both place their father's urn on top of Luka's mom's grave. She's buried at the same fucking cemetery as King's ex. It took Clare months to decide what she wanted to do with her dad's ashes. When Luka suggested instead of scattering his ashes that she should put him on top of his mother, she agreed. I hear car doors opening and peer over my shoulder. At the sight of my brothers and sister walking toward us, a sense of gratefulness overcomes me. My family has welcomed Clare with open arms and them showing up here today is their way of showing Clare their respect. When they reach me, I kiss Car's cheek and shake each of my brother's hands, thanking them for coming.

"How's she doing?" Car quietly asks as we all stand in a line and watch her and Luka say their final goodbyes to their father.

"She's okay. I think she's glad she is finally able to lay him to rest," I say.

"Anyone else find it weird seeing them mourn the loss of a parent, when none of us know what is was like to have one who loved each of us?" Gage's words hang in the air around us as we all digest what he said.

"Tony may not have loved us but the bastard did do one thing right." All of us turn toward Bishop, shooting him a *what the fuck* look. He just shrugs his shoulders and lifts his sunglasses so we can see the serious look in his eyes. "He gave each of us life and that is the only nice thing you will ever catch me saying about that useless cunt." He drops his glasses back into place and fixes his tie like he didn't just say in his own Bishop way that he loves us.

"We love you too, you grumpy fucker," I say in jest, which just earns me a snarl from the big fucker.

"You and Clare coming over for the twins party?" Knight asks me. Now it's my turn to lift my glasses and shoot him a *are you fucking stupid* look.

"Dude, we live next door to you, dumbass, of course we'll be there." King, Gage, Bish and Car laugh while Knight mutters that he should have absorbed me in the womb, making us all laugh harder. We all clamp our mouths closed when Clare and Luka move back and allow the guys to cover the small hole. They thank them before coming toward us. Each of my brothers shake Luka's hand and Car gives him a hug. The guys all whisper words of love as they embrace Clare one after the other. Car suffocates the life out of my girl when it's her turn, and I fight the urge to tear my sister away while waiting for my turn.

"Hi," she whispers as she stands in front of me. Fuck words, they're overrated. I plant a kiss on her lips and tell her without words that I fucking love her and cherish the ground she walks on.

"Dude, we just buried my dad. I'm mourning and don't need to see that shit." Clare and I break apart at the sound of Luka's irritating voice. She smiles sheepishly at her brother.

"I'm grieving too and Rook just made me feel better?" I can't contain my laughter. She elbows me in the stomach which just causes my siblings to join me. Luka storms off, clearly pissed. The guy can't stand the sight of me getting handsy with his sister. Truthfully, I lay it on thick whenever he is around just to fuck with him. "You did that on purpose!" She admonishes me. I throw my arm around her shoulders and lead the way to our car as I answer.

"Sure did, sunshine, he needs to learn you're mine."

LATER THAT NIGHT, me, Gage, King, Knight, Vin and Bishop all sit around the pool with beers in our hands talking shit and celebrating that the twins turning one. It's hard to believe that Havoc and Chaos are growing so fast, and in six months' time, Royal and Channel will be one. Then Meela will be seven... Fuck, time is going by so quickly. I look around at my brothers and Vin, then smirk. We're all shirtless and in our board shorts, each of us now covered in ink. We really do look the part of the mafia family now.

"Anya and I are going to Switzerland for three months." Gage's announcement has all of us focusing on him.

"Why?" King asks.

When a look of uncertainty flashes through his eyes, we all sit forward. "We found a doctor that has a 92% success rate of extracting eggs and inseminating them."

"Wait, but I thought she can't carry a baby?" I ask. Gage cuts a glance to Vin, so naturally we all turn to him.

"She isn't. Carlina is going to carry the baby for them." My jaw hits my fucking lap. I don't know how to describe how I feel but it isn't shock it's... awe. Carlina doing this for them is the most selfless act there is. She is granting Gage and Anya the gift of being parents.

"I... I don't know what to say, man. Congratulations," Bish says as he extends his hand for Gage to shake.

"Thanks, bro. It's scary as hell but we're ready for it. She's it for me. I can't see my life without her, which is why I asked her to marry me this morning." We're all on our feet in seconds and hugging our brother, giving him and his bride to be well wishes.

"A toast." We're all huddled in a circle with our bottles out ready to cheers. "Man I never thought this would ever be our lives. I didn't think any of you ugly fuckers would find beautiful women, that's for sure." We all grumble at Bishop's insult. "Seriously, though, I am so fucking grateful for each of you standing by my side and helping me build this empire for our family. So, cheers to being a Murdoch—" Vin clearing his throat has Bishop snapping his gaze to him and narrowing his eyes playfully.

"Your sister is a Murelo," Vin states proudly. We all groan knowing what is about to come, Bishop has been trying to convince Vin and Car for months to change their names to Murdoch. He says our family name holds weight and Vin's doesn't. Which, then in turn, leads Vin into explaining how he is the Bloodhound and feared by many. Blah blah blah.

"Cheers!" Gage cuts in before these two can get into it. Spending the night with my brothers, drinking and talking shit is something we do regularly now. We each have our second in charge running our territories. I took over the Murelo side for Vin and Car because he needs to travel for work and refused to leave his wife to run things without him. Bish and King were eager to agree with him, thus me now running it. Car, Kiara and Koby run the gym. Anya still has her business in Russia with Vor and Krill. Ally is now a nurse and works at the local hospital and Clare is still studying to be a vet nurse while running her own animal rescue. Thank fuck the rat goes to work with her every day.

All in all, we have a fucking great life. Bishop and Kiara will fly to Miami in a few months to take over for Tony, who is ready to step down so he can spend more time with his daughter and grandson. It's gonna suck them being gone, but at least we own two planes so we can visit often until they move back here. The sound of laughter coming from the back door pulls our attention to the girls. Fuck me dead, each of them is wearing a two piece and fuck my girl looks sexy.

"None of you fuckers are fucking in my pool!" Bishop declares as the girls reach us, making us all laugh. Fuck yeah, this is the life alright. I place a chaste kiss on Clare's lips before smiling down at her.

"I love you, sunshine." Her features soften and she melts into me.

"I love you too. Now, come on, let's go fuck in the pool to piss your brother off."

"I fucking heard that!" Bishop scolds, making me laugh

so fucking hard tears leak from my eyes. I fucking love my family.

Epilogue

Royal

19 years later....

I'm so fucking over having to do this school shit. Dad refuses to allow us to join the family business and said we all have to go to college!

Why would the heirs to the biggest mafia family in the continental US have to go to college, you ask?

Because our moms told our dads they didn't want us involved in the business and wanted us to be free to choose what we want to do. We all may be cousins, but we're close like siblings. Well, the four of us are. We all applied to the same college and given who we are, we knew we would get in. If not on our own merit, our parents would have paid our way in.

"Stop fucking pouting. We have six months of school left and then we're out of here." I glare at the asshole as he reclines back on my bed, tosses a football into the air then catches it. Unlike me, Chaos doesn't want to join the family business. He wants to go pro and get drafted into the NFL.

"Fuck you! None of this shit is gonna matter when I take over," I state in a matter-of-fact tone. It's true what I say, I am the one who is going to take over and lead this family when my dad steps down.

"Calm down, Royal. We all know you're the future king of the family and all that shit." I glare at Havoc as he saunters back into the room with a towel wrapped around his waste, water dripping everywhere.

"You're leaving footprints on my carpet!" I scold. The asshole comes closer and shakes his hair, flicking water droplets all over me. Chaos laughs at his stupid ass twin. I strike out and punch the asshole right in arm.

"You sound like Aunt Ally. *You boys stop playing ball in the house.*" We all laugh at his impression of our aunt. We haven't been home in a long time, the last time was months ago to celebrate Meela graduating and becoming a doctor. She is crazy fucking smart but, due to the age gap between her and the four of us, we never really hung out much. Destiny is three years younger than us, she's seventeen. Uncle Gage and Aunt Anya are pushing her to become a lawyer but Dest isn't having any of that and wants to be an MMA fighter. We all know secretly Uncle G is thrilled at the idea. Nytress and Unique are fifteen and sixteen and only care about cheerleading. Uncle Rook is trying to convince them that they don't need college and to stay home with him. Honestly, my poor cousins are going to rebel so hard when they finally get their freedom from their dad.

The door to my dorm bursts open and Channel rushes in with a panicked look in her eyes. Havoc, Chaos and I are on her in seconds.

"What happened?"

"Who did it?"

"Are you hurt?" we all ask at the same time. She shakes her head and pushes through us and rushes to my bed-side table, grabs the remote and flicks the TV on turning it straight to the news.

"Channel—"

She cuts me off. "Shut up and listen, Royal." She turns the volume up and the three of us creep in closer to see what has her panties in a twist.

"Just in, the plane that alleged mafia boss, Bishop Murdoch and his brothers, King, Knight, Rook, Gage and his brother-in-law Vincent Murelo, were traveling on from Miami to New York has gone down." My heart stops. *"Police and fire were first to the scene and sources say the bodies of the six passengers have not been located, leaving the other four crew members injured and in critical care. The captain and co-captain didn't make it. Now over to Jenny who has local police chief with her. Jenny."* The camera switches over to another woman who stands with the wrecked plane at her back and a man in a police uniform beside her.

"Thank you, Kelly, I'm here with police chief Lawrence. What can you tell us about the missing passengers?"

"We've found five sets of tire tracks that come in one way and out another. We believe that the six passengers have been taken and that this isn't some random crash. We believe this flight was targeted— My cell ringing pulls me away from the TV. When I see my mom's name, I quickly answer it.

"Mom, what the hell is going on?" I snap instead of a greeting.

"Royal, it's your father–" My mom is one of toughest people I know and she isn't scared of shit, she can make my father bend to her will with one look. Hearing the fear in her voice has me clutching the phone so tight I fear I'll snap it. When the others crowd around me, I put it on speaker phone. "The plane went down and they–"

"I know, we just saw it on the news," I say cutting her off.

"You and your cousins need to get on the next flight out of Utah and come home." The four of us exchanged a loaded look before I ask.

"What the hell is going on, Mom, tell me the truth." My voice is cold and emotionless. Whenever I panic or worry, I'm somehow able to shut all my emotions off and feel nothing. It's a blessing for me and it will be a curse for the fuckers that took my father, I'll kill them all.

"I just received a video, your father and uncles have been taken by a cousin of mine I didn't even know I existed."

"I thought grandpa killed all your family?"

"We did as well, son. Apparently he missed one and now he has come after us." Hearing her sniffle and know she is crying kills me to not be there with her.

"We'll kill the son of a bitch for thinking he could ever fuck with our family," Chaos snarls and the rest of us hum our agreement.

"That's all well and good, except the bastard is the governor of Miami!" I shoot each of my cousins a look asking if they are ready for what is about to happen. Each of them nod.

"We'll be on the next flight out," I growl.

"Royal?"

"Yeah, Mom?"

"I won't survive losing him," she sobs. My mom loves my dad with every beat of her heart, their love makes me never want to settle for anything less. They have set the bar so high that I fear no woman will ever reach it.

"You won't have to, I'm my father's son and I swear to you, I'll burn the fucking city to the ground until I find the bastard who dared to fuck with us. We are the Murdoch's and we never fucking give up!"

Want more from the Murdoch's?
Click the link below,
Stalemate

Thank You!

Holy shitballs!
That's it, this is the final book in the Murdoch Mafia series!
This time I mean it, there is no more hidden books like
Rook's. Each of these guys and girls got their happily ever
after so it is time to let them rest, for now... I may be
tempted to write the next generation? What do you think of
that possibility, let me know.
This is such a bittersweet feeling for me. I have loved going
on these wild ass rides with each of these couples, I'm sad
that it is over.
I'm gonna miss them so much but... all good things must
come to an end and I have other books I need to finish
writing and get out this year!
Thank you so much for reading Rook and Clare's book, it
means more than you will ever know.
I appreciate you taking the time to read this whole series, if
you loved Rook and Clare's book, please leave a review on
Amazon, Bookbub or Goodreads.
Reviews are like tips for us authors, the more reviews we get
the more exposure the book gets.

**If you want to stay up to date with all my new
releases follow me on Facebook and Instagram**

Mafia Romance

<u>Murdoch Mafia Series</u>

Played By The Bishop

Tormented By The King

Tortured By The Knight

Tempted By The Queen

Turned By The Pawn

Ruined By The Rook

<u>Murdoch Mafia Novella</u>

Stalemate

<u>Memento Mori Series</u>

Reign Of Royal

Broken By Sin

In Havoc Lays Chaos

<u>Godfathers of the night</u>

London has Fallen

Damned By His Angel

<u>Re Della Strada</u>

Shattered Soul

Fractured Heart

Tainted Essence

<u>Fairytales With A Twist</u>

Condemned Beast

Secret Society/ Bully

Filthy Few

Forever Filthy

Filthiest Of Them All

Masked Men Novella (Pure Smut)

Dirty Priest

Dirty Daddy

Sports Romance

<u>Playing For Keeps</u>

Offside

Touchdown

End Game

Hail Mary

Blindside

RH Sports

Hate Us Like You Mean It

MM

Love Me Like You Mean It

Paranormal Romance

<u>The Veil Of Obsidian</u>

Of Time And Carnage

<u>Curse Of Fate</u>

Dream

Fate

Nightmare

Redemption

Anarchy

Brutal Savages

Savage Lies

Brutal Truth

Savage Beast

Brutal Beauty

ACKNOWLEDGMENTS

Holy shit, it may take me some time to get through this list because this series was hard to write, plot and bring together. It took a whole lot of people and I need to thank each of them for their help and guidance.

First, Marcus, my lover, my best friend, my Bishop. You inspire me daily to write these love stories and happily ever after's because, baby, I didn't believe in either of those things until I met you! Because of you, I am living my happily ever after every single day, I love you more than words can express. Just don't let your dick slip or we may need to send your ass to Russia!

Second, Natasha, you are a bossy bitch who drives over to my house to yell at me and scare the shit out of me just so I will write. I fucking love you for that! Thank you for pushing me to jump genres and take a chance at writing something other than PNR.

Third, Clare-bear, lady I fucking adore you and how passionate you are about each of the character's I write. When I knew Book was getting a book your name popped right into my head and therefore, Clare Santiago was born and is named after you!

Fourth, Lizz, my bomb ass editor who makes these books shine like a fucking diamond! THANK YOU! I wish I could put into words how grateful I am for you, I'm so blessed to have met you. I can't wait to keep working together on my next projects, you truly are a sweetheart.

Fifth, my demon slayers, my children, my heart, my everything. I love you both more than you will ever know. Thank you for being so good while Mummy was writing each of these books and being my mini hype team. I love you both with everything that I am.

Sixth, my ARC team! You ladies are fucking amazing, I honest to God could not have done these books without you all hyping me the hell up and demanding more from me. You ladies are the real MVP's. Ash, Lora, Debbie, Kahanna, Amber, Jasmine, Katelyn, Kylie, Lynzi, Melissa, Nadine, Sarah and Cyndi, I love you ladies!

Seventh, my mummy, my daddy, and my bonus dad. You three are a driving force. The need to make you proud of me pushes to write these books. I know you all are proud of me already but I never want to let you down. Thank you for loving me and supporting on this crazy as hell ride.

Eighth, Jaye Pratt, thank you so much lovely for formatting these books and making these dope as fuck headers for each of these books. I am indebted to you and happy to be your guinea pig anytime.

Ninth, Leah, my girl! Thank you, babe, thank you thank you, thank you for making these bomb as fuck covers for this whole series and all the graphics. You are incredibly talented and I am truly in awe of you. Thank you doesn't seem enough, so the sport romance is for you, babes, keep an eye out.

Tenth, my readers, thank you from the bottom of my heart for reading my book. Without you none of this would have been possible. I wouldn't be able to live out my dream if it wasn't for each of you so thank you, thank you, thank you.

Xxxx

Sam

ABOUT THE AUTHOR

Samantha Barrett is a dark romance, PNR author who loves to write out-of-the-box stories. She is originally from the land of the long white cloud, New Zealand. She is totally fluking her way through this whole author gig, if she isn't writing you can find her kicking back with her kids and husband with a bag of chips and a glass of wine in her hand. Sam loves Twilight and is a TWIHARD proudly.